Fishing for hun
in a boiling sea

Bolan moved toward the dock.

A sentry burst from cover, his AK-47 scattering 7.62mm gut-rippers from the hip.

Bolan's huge handgun boomed in anger. The sentry's rifle flew from his hands as though snatched by supernatural forces.

The AutoMag thundered again. The 240-grain skull-buster blasted the enemy's brain apart.

More troops appeared. Bolan brought the M-3 into play. His trigger finger tightened. The M-3 chattered until its thirty-round vocabulary was exhausted.

No man was eager to test the silence. . . .

Also available from Gold Eagle Books, publishers of the Executioner series:

Mack Bolan's
ABLE TEAM

Mack Bolan's
PHOENIX FORCE

MACK BOLAN

THE EXECUTIONER 56

BOLAN

Island Deathtrap

A GOLD EAGLE BOOK FROM

W🌐RLDWIDE

TORONTO · NEW YORK · LONDON · PARIS
AMSTERDAM · STOCKHOLM · HAMBURG
ATHENS · MILAN · TOKYO · SYDNEY

Dedicated to the "River Rats" who flew in the Red
River Valley of North Vietnam and encountered
the most heavily defended airspace in the history
of aerial warfare. Many of those who did not come
home are still listed as Missing in Action.

First edition August 1983

Special thanks and acknowledgment to
E. Richard Churchill for his contributions to this work.

ISBN 0-373-61056-4

Copyright © 1983 by Worldwide Library.
Philippine copyright 1983. Australian copyright 1983.

All rights reserved. Except for use in any review, the
reproduction or utilization of this work in whole or in part
in any form by any electronic, mechanical or other means,
now known or hereafter invented, including xerography,
photocopying and recording, or in any information storage
or retrieval system, is forbidden without the permission
of the publisher, Worldwide Library, 225 Duncan Mill Road,
Don Mills, Ontario, Canada M3B 3K9. All the characters in
this book have no existence outside the imagination of the
author and have no relation whatsoever to anyone bearing the
same name or names. They are not even distantly inspired by
any individual known or unknown to the author, and all the
incidents are pure invention.

The Gold Eagle trademark, consisting of the words
GOLD EAGLE and the portrayal of an eagle, and the
Worldwide trademark, consisting of the word
WORLDWIDE in which the letter "O" is represented by a
depiction of a globe, are trademarks of Worldwide Library.

Printed in Canada

1

"The whole community is terrorized," Hal Brognola said.

"That's what this guy Ed Warner tells us. According to him, there's no local law enforcement in Kenlandport, Maine. The population is about fifty all told, and most of them are elderly or a few families with kids. The families are practically all interrelated, and they usually handle their own problems. Now they're all scared out of their wits. Neighbor doesn't talk to neighbor. People are afraid to do anything for fear of what may happen.

"Nevertheless, the county sheriff doesn't see any problem. Same goes for the state police. The Boston office of the FBI finally sent a report forward after Warner kept bugging them. They said there might be some basis for a possible civil rights violation and conspiracy.

"Well, I guess that's about the size of it from what we know."

Hal spread his hands, drumming his fingertips on the table a few times. Then he withdrew the half-smoked, well-chewed cigar from the corner of his mouth. "Think it's something we should look into?"

Mack Bolan communicated his decision with a flash of his blue eyes.

"Do we have contact ability?" he asked.

Hal nodded. "Affirmative."

"Tell this Ed Warner that John Phoenix will be in touch. I'll need his description for a positive ID."

"Got it from the reporting agent in Boston," April Rose told him. Without being asked she continued, "There are two commercial airports Jack Grimaldi can use. Portland or Bangor."

Bolan drew a mental image of the state of Maine. "I'll go with Portland."

"Then I'll have land transport waiting," April promised.

Mack fixed Hal with his gaze. "Any further intel to add?"

"There are some unsubstantiated reports that a new conduit has recently opened to move hardcases in and out of the country. Also, New Jersey law officers report that Big Jim Lane hasn't been spotted locally in nearly a month."

"He's in import-export, isn't he?"

"Only when the cost of people-moving is high enough to attract him. Armory theft is more his bag. He's got a rep as a supplier of hot military arms. Big Jim has some fast boats he uses to make deliveries of stolen arms and munitions at sea."

Bolan filed the information.

April's voice cut into his thoughts. "Jack has his rotors turning. He'll lift you off from Stony Man in minutes."

"Thanks," Bolan said as he stood up. "If Warner's been making that much noise, I don't have much time."

April watched her man leave the room. There was never enough time. Never.

But she let him rush away, and gladly.

From his recent attitude, she knew that Mack now hankered for a life that only he, The Executioner, controlled. She could tell he itched to act solo again, as in the old days when he operated outside of the law as a scourge to his enemies.

April's serious wounding in Europe on Mack's most recent mission particularly distressed the big guy, and she knew it. He had been horrified at her close call with death, brooded alone for hours on their return to Stony Man Farm, finally confided to her a deep need to pursue his life's path independent of comrades, support systems, government agencies, the government itself.

He wanted—needed—to go it alone again.

"Mack responded fast on this one because he wants out," she told Hal.

"What do you mean? Is this woman's intuition talking?"

"Mack wants to go back to where he belongs," she murmured in reply. "He's searching. He wants to find his own America. He wants to act one on one, be responsible for his own actions. I think he's readying himself for being on his own again."

"Professionally," Hal said, "I discount your views because of your convalescence—your health could be marring your judgment. But personally," he added, "I believe you may be right, April. We both knew Mack when he was on the lam, a renegade, and there's something in him now that reminds me of that. Think we ought to interfere?"

"Hal, his commitment to justice has never been stronger," she replied. "Let him go to Maine. Let him go to the furthest edge. On his own. Let him find himself. Let him find himself. I want to see him as he really is, at his best...."

2

It was as though the tentacles of mist sought the source of the death smell.

The closed front door and destroyed screen of the kitchen window posed no barrier to the pervasive gray dampness. In the small living and sleeping area, Mack Bolan allowed his light free play. The thin beam's intensity was slightly diminished as the fingers of fog intruded into the two-room shack.

The room had been searched. How much of the clutter was the result of a hunt for information and how much was the normal environment of a lonely man's life-style, Bolan could not tell. Books were pulled from shelving along the north wall and dumped carelessly on the floor. The homemade shelving had obviously been constructed over a period of time as the need arose.

With the toe of his rubber-soled black canvas shoe, Bolan flipped over several volumes. The majority of the books indicated an interest in world history. A variety of newsmagazines added to the mess. Half a dozen copies of area newspapers were thrown around. Ed Warner had been a well-read guy.

Bolan let his beam scan the room again. There was

no television set. He recalled seeing a radio on the kitchen counter. The scattered books and the lack of a TV said something about Ed Warner.

The dead man's tenacity made another statement about him. According to Hal Brognola, Ed's attempts at gaining aid for his home community were frustrated at every turn.

Bolan remembered that there was no local law enforcement in Kenlandport. It was a closed, secluded settlement, typical of the far northern New England coast, in which the area's citizens cared for their own. Yeah, and repulsed outsiders when the need arose.

Unless the outsiders proved more than a match for the limited resources of the locals.... It was apparently such a failing that had pushed Ed Warner to go in search of outside help.

According to Hal, the county officials viewed the situation as one rating minimal concern. Hal had spoken to the county sheriff, and Bolan remembered the Maine lawman's words as transcribed from that phone call:

A certain number of fights and the like are nor mal in any town. Besides, nobody's been really hurt. Nobody's dead. At least no murders have been reported. For that matter, Ed Warner is no saint himself, you know. The way we see it, he's most likely gotten in over his head in some sort of family squabble. Best just let them work it out. That's the way we do things up here. The

people of Kenlandport don't hold much with outsiders getting involved.

The state police had said pretty much the same.
Hal's transcription reported that they had heard of
some local problems. But even Ed Warner admitted
to the state investigator that the situation involved
not much more than vandalism and threats. And yes,
Ed agreed, no one was dead. At least not yet.

Legally, the FBI had no jurisdiction in matters
of this kind, but as a result of Warner's persis-
tent nagging, the Boston office did send a report
that eventually reached Hal. However, by the time
Mack Bolan responded to the plea for help, it
was too late. At least for Ed Warner. He was a guy
who did not give up when he believed he was right,
no matter what the cost. He did not stop until they
killed him. Bolan could understand that kind of
man.

Mack could all but see the guy take his pride in hand
like a hat and ask total strangers for their help. Yeah,
and then endure the frustration of being turned away.
The cost to the independent Ed Warner must have
been enormous.

The warrior in nightfighter black glanced back into
the kitchen. The bloody, tortured heap that was once a
living person indicated the cost was even higher than
Warner could have anticipated.

Bolan moved across the room and let the flashlight's beam explore the place's only closet. The clothing hanging there was clean but showed signs of hav-

ing been worn well and often. A single jacket, long out of style, hung atop a pair of carefully pressed trousers. Had Ed worn them when he visited the various agencies? Bolan suspected he had.

He turned away from the closet. Outside, the fog had thickened. From where he stood Bolan could only barely make out the bulk of a tree trunk near the edge of the small front stoop.

Again Bolan's flashlight swept the room. There was nothing to detain him further. Kenlandport, up the coast a bit to the north, seemed his only choice. But getting the closemouthed locals to open up without Warner to introduce him might be something else again.

Suddenly Bolan heard something. It was not close, but it was approaching. He looked outside again but could not see for the fog. Bolan let his sense of hearing chart the observer's approach. Now he judged the unseen presence to be about thirty feet north and east of the front stoop.

Bolan let his hand fill with the silenced might of the Beretta 93-R. His small flashlight died at a touch of its switch. Bolan let his total nightvision develop in the abrupt darkness.

Faint rustlings among the fallen leaves and twigs at the fringe of the woods indicated the watcher's impatience.

Bolan figured it would be impolite to keep his visitor waiting any longer.

Crouching low, becoming a three-dimensional shadow in the thick fog, Mack Bolan rushed outside and dived over the splintered wood of the weatherbeaten front stoop.

His mind registered a passing tug at his right ankle. The early night erupted in a flash of light and an explosion of sound directly over his head.

3

Bolan recognized the shotgun's thunder and flash. Both barrels of the twelve-gauge had roared out their fury as one. Whoever set the trip-cord trap had also wired the twin triggers together.

Only his combat instinct to move low had saved him.

Unmoving, Bolan felt with his free hand for the cord entangled around his ankle. From touch he identified the material. It was nylon fishing leader. Thin, tough, all but invisible, it was ideal trip wire.

Bolan untangled himself and lay motionless. The restless foot stirrings continued nearby. The soft whispers of sound he could detect were those of someone uncertain how to proceed. Bolan decided the next move was up to his hidden adversary. The waiting was hell, but the matter would soon be resolved. With the Beretta in his hand, Bolan remained curled up on the damp earth, listening. Waiting. His knees were drawn up, his shoes firmly implanted on a rise in the ground. Mack Bolan was poised and ready to spring.

The beam of light Bolan expected finally came. It

was broad and dim to the point of being practically useless.

The light's holder moved closer. The faint light circled Bolan's body, then moved to center on his back. The light moved toward him. One step. Two steps. Three steps. *Now!*

The man in black uncoiled like a snake striking at unsuspecting prey. Bolan's muscular left arm swept the other's feet off the ground in one powerful backhand swing. His legs straightened in a single driving motion. His shoulder hit the off-balance body at mid-thigh.

As the pair crashed to the ground together, Bolan's left hand sought and found the other's throat. The business end of the Beretta's small silencer came to rest firmly against the center of the forehead of the stunned loser.

"Move and you die," Bolan said. His voice was devoid of emotion.

"Go to hell!" It was the voice of a male, past the age of childhood but not yet a man.

Beneath his hand, Bolan felt throat muscles work. He slid the Beretta into its leather holster and did a quick weapons check on his captive. The only potentially dangerous object the youth carried was a long clasp knife. Bolan pocketed it and allowed the boy to sit up.

"Are you going to kill me now or do you plan to use the end of a cigarette on me for an hour or so first?" The young-old voice was thick with barely suppressed fear.

Bolan switched on his flashlight. He played the beam quickly over the face of the youth.

Seventeen, eighteen at most, the kid had deep brown eyes that looked almost black in the darkness. Without letting the light blind the boy, Bolan studied his face, then his body.

The kid was thin. But he was wiry thin, with the tough slenderness of one who worked hard and did not bitch. His hands were almost delicate, the tapered fingers possibly those of a musician or artist. But it was the eyes that drew Bolan's complete attention. They were truly windows to the youth's soul. They were, he realized, the eyes of one who could love deeply or hate unrelentingly.

The boy suddenly exploded into a frenzy of motion.

Bolan knew his physical assessment of the teenager had been correct. For seconds the two struggled. The only sounds of their intense conflict came from dislodged twigs and bits of ground cover.

Bolan's physical size and strength brought the unequal contest to a panting end for the kid. His voice was full of frustration and humiliation at having been so quickly overpowered.

"You better kill me now, mister. After the way you and your pals destroyed Uncle Ed, you best just kill me right off. If I ever get loose from you, I'll sure as God pay you back for what you did to him."

"Were you the one who rigged that double-barreled twelve?"

"Go to hell!"

"I'm not your enemy. I came to help. Your uncle—if he's Ed Warner—asked for help."

"Okay, you know his name. That proves nothing."

Bolan relaxed the pressure on the kid's bent arm. He had too much to do in too little time to have another wrestling match with this fiery kid.

"I only got word this morning. Your uncle just didn't know who to tell and how to get word to us." Bolan felt no need to explain his actions or to justify his presence. Yet he wanted the hurt, angry, betrayed kid to know the truth. Some spark that glowed from within the boy indicated it would be effort well spent.

"You sure took your time getting here."

The boy's tone, if not his words, indicated a softening in attitude.

"My name is John Phoenix."

"You FBI?"

"No. I don't belong to any organization that you're aware of," Bolan answered truthfully. Then he added cryptically, "I don't belong to anything. Think of me as justice."

"Rick Cartright," said the youth, calmed by the words of the blacksuited apparition. "Ed was my uncle. My mother's brother. He sort of looked out for me."

Bolan did not press the matter. In his own good time Rick would or would not explain his personal circumstances.

"Let's get up now," Bolan said. "We've got things to do."

As one, the two came to their feet. Both brushed themselves free of clinging bits of the forest floor.

"I'd like my knife back, please."

Bolan returned the pocket weapon. He heard the sound of the knife going back into the kid's belt; it was one of the many sounds in the fog that reminded Bolan of his own youth.

"Did you see any of the men who murdered your uncle?"

"No. At least not for sure. You don't think I'd have let them do that to him if I'd seen them?"

"But you have seen the people you think may have been responsible," Bolan prodded.

"Yeah. Everyone's seen them. It was only Uncle Ed who had the nerve to try to do anything about them."

"Where can I find these people?"

"You really mean to do them in, don't you?"

"If you tell me where to find them."

"They have a stronghold out on the island. It's called Eagle Nest Island, though there hasn't been an eagle there since before I was born. It's out about a mile or so from Kenlandport Bay."

"How far is the bay from here?" asked Bolan.

"Half a mile at most."

"We don't need my car. Let's go."

To their right, the incoming tide lapped the rocky shore. A gull screamed its protest at the worsening fog and the approaching night.

The woods threatened to advance across the narrow shore to meet the incoming sea. A suggestion of evening breeze sighed through the tops of the taller trees. Close to the ground the tangle of brushy undergrowth served to bar all but the most determined.

Bolan and the kid covered less than a hundred yards when a shadowy figure clutching a shotgun rose from the gloom. There was no mistaking the threat posed by the dark outline of man and weapon.

"Friend?" Bolan whispered to the youth, his voice low but intense.

Rick peered into the mist. "No way."

The Beretta again left leather to breathe the damp air of coming night.

"You two lost or something?" It was the bullying voice of one accustomed to having his way. Bolan placed the accent as no farther north than New Jersey.

Without waiting for a command from Bolan, Rick answered for both of them.

"We're just on our way back to Kenlandport. We're late." His flat Maine twang was in sharp contrast to the Mid-Atlantic inflections of the guy with the automatic shotgun.

The narrowing distance between them became critical. The time for choosing was all but past. The man blocking their path made the decision on his own.

"I heard a twelve-gauge let go a few minutes ago. You know you hicks were told to turn in your weapons. I guess you backwoods 'billies need a little help in understanding plain English. Get up here where I can see you.''

The autoloading twelve-gauge began to swing forward. It viewed Bolan and the kid in its single staring eye. With that motion the guy made an unscheduled appointment with dark and silent death.

The Beretta sighed twice in response to a pair of quick tightenings of Bolan's trigger finger. Without ever realizing it took more than six twelve-gauge shells and tough talk to make him a man, the guy started to drop, his knees refusing to support his weight. He sank to the rocks of the shore.

Rick advanced on shaky legs toward the corpse. His weak light came to life and cast its faint beam down onto the dead man.

Bolan heard the kid's sharp intake of breath. Death is final. It is never pretty and seldom pleasant. A youth capable of viewing the effects of violent death and remaining unmoved would not be someone Bolan could trust at his side. Or at his back. Rick Cartright passed a test he was unaware he had taken.

''My God, Mr. Phoenix. You got him right in the center of his chest.'' The dim light wavered. ''And through the nose.''

The kid circled the downed body. Bolan heard some small rocks go flying as Rick slipped, then he saw the weak beam of light directed at the kid's feet.

''Oh, my God! His brains are scattered all over these rocks! I slipped on his brains!''

Without warning, the light switched off. Bolan followed the boy's stumbling progress with his ears.

After eight or ten steps, the kid halted. Sounds of retching destroyed the calm.

Bolan gave the kid time enough to get over the worst of it before moving to stand by his side. He dropped his big hand to Rick's lean shoulder.

"Ready?"

The single word was enough. The kid stood and nodded, wiping at his mouth with the back of his hand.

Again the pair moved north toward Kenlandport.

"You have one hell of a fast draw," Rick said after they had walked in silence for a few minutes. "How did you know you could beat him to the punch?" The words tumbled from his lips as if to disguise what the kid viewed as his own weakness.

"I didn't outdraw him. My hand was filled before he ever became a threat."

They continued to cover ground. Again the Executioner spoke. "The time to unholster a weapon is before it's needed. Not after. After may be too late. If you want to survive, that is."

It was a short but vital speech. Bolan could only trust that the kid understood.

When the two of them rounded a slight jutting of the shore, Kenlandport came into view. Seen only as a scattered cluster of dim lights, the village was not impressive. Each of the fifteen or so lights was an indistinct, yellow orange glow. If anything, the fog was thicker here on the little bay.

The youth spoke. "We've got to get a boat—if

you're really serious about getting those guys on the island.''

"I'm serious," Bolan said.

Again the pair moved ahead. From their left, animal sounds cut through the fog and dark.

"Pigs," Rick explained. "They're upset. Do we have time to see what's bothering them?"

They didn't, but Bolan said it would be all right. Long ago he had learned not to overlook anything, however trivial it might seem. If the youth felt the grunting and squealing of the animals was worth checking, it was worth a few minutes of their time.

Rick's light swept the solidly built enclosure that housed perhaps eight or ten huge sows.

"They haven't been fed. That's because Becky isn't here."

"Becky?"

"Becky Devereaux. She's a friend."

Rick's tone alerted Bolan.

"You said Becky isn't here. Where is she?"

"Her grandmother said she went up to Bangor to visit an aunt. I can't buy that. Becky takes care of these pigs, and she's real responsible. She wouldn't go on a visit without having someone feed and water them. And she wouldn't leave without telling me."

"How old is Becky?" Bolan asked.

"Fifteen. Going on sixteen."

"And you like her."

The kid hesitated. "I love her." His words were uttered flatly. They left no room for misunderstanding.

"If you don't think Becky's in Bangor, where do you think she is?"

Rick located a sack of cracked corn before he answered.

"I think they have Becky." He jerked his head in the direction of the bay. "Her grandfather owns the best diesel trawler along this stretch of coast."

Rick scattered a five-gallon bucket of feed along the length of a worn and empty trough. Instantly the immense sows began to shoulder one another aside in an effort to fill empty bellies. White teeth in massive mouths slashed at one another as the hungry animals pushed and shoved. The angry gruntings were lessened as powerful jaws chomped on the welcome grain.

"Does Becky like these pigs?"

The kid shrugged his thin shoulders. "She understands them. That's why I know she didn't just up and go to Bangor. She wouldn't do that to them."

A question tugged at Bolan's mind.

"How many people know the way you feel about Becky?"

"It's the way we feel about each other, sir. Not all that many. Uncle Ed knew. Becky's grandfather probably suspects." He turned back to look at the animals.

"Time's getting away from us," Bolan prompted.

"Right. Let's see if I can't rustle up a boat. It will have to be a dory. I'll row us out to the island."

Bolan would have preferred making his initial probe alone. At the same time he could not justify a refusal that would limit Rick's participation. The kid had a lot at stake. He deserved the right to lend a hand.

With the slightly built shadow leading the way, the two figures moved again toward whatever awaited them.

4

Bolan was glad to be back in the remote regions, isolated from the cities.

For the moment, he had had it with the "big time" of international counterterrorism.

It was good to be back in the true heartland of his country, which was wherever the individual could face hardship on his or her own, without benefit of government interference of any sort.

On the rocky coastland of Maine, despite the rumblings of trouble he felt here, and despite the vulnerability of such an area *because* of its freedom from any involvement by the authorities, Bolan knew he moved among his kind of people.

The Laser Wagon was garaged after its test run in Europe; Stony Man Farm continued to hum through day and night in its mission to prey upon political killers everywhere; and the huge machine of Mack Bolan's heavily soldiered effort to scourge the world of terror was in high gear and advancing inexorably.

But sometimes Mack felt no part of it.

The human being that was The Executioner understood the danger of the supreme power that he wielded. The danger was not only a threat to his enemies, it also menaced himself and his allies.

The blitzing Able Team and Phoenix Force overkill that he and Hal had unleashed against Yoshida's troika and the forces of Hydra, in one of the biggest battle events of modern times, threatened by its very victory to dehumanize the victors into overconfident killing machines. Bolan smelled the bad odor of that possibility and it turned him off such supreme power.

The logic of the danger was apparent to him on every mission. His campaign against Paradine, for example, included the use of the Laser Lok scope for ultimate accuracy. But had the device, finally, saved April Rose from being hit? No.

In an earlier mission, Bolan had secretly and only briefly used the first-ever 9mm AutoMag, a double-action, stainless-steel weapon from Wildey, with vent rib and fixed barrel, that could shoot fifteen rounds of 9mm Winchester "big-game" Magnums. Was the new piece worth it, compared with his faithful Big Thunder? At a purchase price of $5000 with all the trimmings, probably not. He had put the gun into storage.

Mack Bolan preferred to trust his own combat experience, not just the top-of-the-line toys that were so easily available through his organization. The time was inevitably approaching when he would free himself from his sanctioned backup and approach his world of fire and fury by himself.

He could feel in his chilled bones the rumblings of

such a change as he paced through the twilight fog of Kenlandport's remote and private world.

He loved all the men and women of Stony Man Farm like his own family, and it was for that reason that Bolan could not endanger them by allowing the organization to get mightier and more powerful than each of the individuals who operated it.

"Perfection is the enemy of the good," said the French thinker Voltaire. What he meant was that power corrupts, that success can lead to self-destruction.

A man is made hard by hardship, and that was the way Mack Bolan intended to proceed.

By hardship.

There was a time in the bloody campaign against Yoshida when Bolan thought his ruthless drive into zones that were forbidden would put his fighters beyond the pale of government sanction forever. And that thought, although it had disturbed him because of his love for his warriors, nevertheless enlivened his mind and brought forth a resurgence of energy within his commitment to war everlasting. For it reminded him of the days when he had fought the Mafia outside of the law; it brought back the sensation of dealing out justice while simultaneously fending off the powerhouse of law enforcement.

And he liked that sensation.

It brought him home, back to his psychological roots as a sniper, as a stony man whose doctrine was *personal* war.

Prowling now into the unknown with a young man

called Rick, in one of the more obscure coastal havens of America's northeast, produced these latest thoughts within Bolan. He welcomed the thoughts. They helped him define his direction on his third mile. Already he owed more to Rick, and to the real people he represented, than the young man would ever know.

All this, even before the battle had begun....

5

"That's Eagle Nest Island." The kid's outstretched arm directed Bolan's keen gaze.

The island crouched low on the near horizon about a mile away. Faint flickers of light appeared and vanished.

"Fog's really coming in pretty thick now, but you can see the lights on the island."

"How big is it?"

"The island's about four hundred yards north to south. Maybe a thousand east to west. The trees come right down to the shore on all sides, and there are some pretty big rocks in lots of places. The only good landing site is on the south side about midway around. That's where those lights are."

"How are the rocks on the north side—on the opposite side of the island from the lights?" Bolan asked.

"Bad. About as bad as anywhere except the point at the east end."

"Could you set me ashore on the north side?"

"You don't scare easy, do you?"

"No."

"It's up to you. Yep, I can set you ashore there,

but lots of really brave people get chicken when the
waves start banging them against the rocks.''

"And pick me up later?"

"I said I could." His voice carried a statement of
fact, not a boast. To the kid it was unthinkable that
he would put Bolan ashore and not stand by to ferry
him back. Bolan realized the kid saw the total picture
and he liked that kind of vision.

The chuffing of a diesel carried through the mist.

"Boat coming." Rick cocked his head to hear better. "Probably a lobsterman coming in. More than
likely one of the guys who caved in and is running his
boat for those bastards on the island."

"Doing what?"

"Meeting ships out at sea. Bringing people in.
Taking others out. No one wants to talk about it. As
though silence makes wrong into right."

Yeah, it was pretty much the way Hal and April
Rose doped it out. What better place than the isolated coast of Maine to become a safe conduit for those
who did not want to attempt entry or exit through
normal channels?

And what more logical way to ensure cooperation
of the local citizens than to threaten their wives and
families?

It was the warped and twisted logic of those who
lived off the fear of others.

The arrival of the diesel right on the heels of their
encounter with the goon on the shore might be just
coincidence. It might also be the result of a radioed
report of the earlier shotgun blast back at Warner's

shack. Bolan viewed coincidence as unlikely. It was that sort of thinking that kept the Executioner alive.

"Rick, I need some stuff from my car. I want to check out some things. Will you get my car and drive it back here?"

"You trust me with your car and equipment?"

"Only as far as you trust yourself."

"Do you have the keys?" Bolan caught the change in the kid's inflection. Trust meant much to the lean Rick Cartright.

"Stuck in the tailpipe."

Without further comment the kid left the shore. He was lost to Bolan's sight within seconds. The sound of the kid's deck shoes crunching on the ground cover continued longer.

Moving rapidly but cautiously, the man in black let his ears lead him to the diesel's landing site. A spotlight mounted on the boat's oak bow probed the growing dark. It acted as a homing signal for Bolan.

"Watch it! Can't see a damn thing in this fog. Easy now. We're about there," came the words from the boat.

The engine slowed in response.

Fingers of fog parted to allow Bolan a quick glimpse of the incoming craft. Two men stood at the bow. At least one more was out of view where he manned the wheel in the tiny cabin at the stern.

"Easy. Don't want to sink this tub."

Once more the spotlight probed. This time it located what it sought. The man directing it let the light cling like a leech to an ancient pier. Little more than a walkway, the plank and pile construction extended no more than ten yards into the bay.

The guy stopped directing the light and reached for a line. The moment the spotlight swung free, Bolan caught the quick glint of light on gunmetal. A pair of Uzis and some side arms was his instant assessment. So much for the possibility that a lobsterman was returning late.

Bolan stepped onto the shore end of the ramshackle pier and moved to meet the newcomers.

The craft's worn bow nuzzled the nearest planks as the line was tossed awkwardly toward the top of the mossy piling. The loop missed and fell into the sea.

"Dammit!"

"Come on," ordered a voice from the stern. "Hank said he needed backup. Let's give it to him."

A fraction too late, the man at the helm reversed the idling engine. The missed cast of the line and the tardy reverse of the slowly turning prop allowed the boat to continue along the side of the pier. Bumpers made of worn auto tires scraped against the gray green pilings.

Aware of what was happening, the helmsman increased the flow of fuel to the nearly quiet engine. The propeller began to thrash in the water, and Bolan made his move.

No more than ten yards separated him from the bow when he called out.

"Hank sent you a message!"

Bolan could all but feel the surprise his words evoked. An unseen hand groped for and found the spotlight's handle. The beam of light began to rise from where it pointed down toward the sea.

The 93-R gently coughed, and life gave way to death for the guy manning the light. The spot swung upward as the man fell, and Bolan noted a chunk of skull torn free and sent toward the boat's stern. The guy had just received Hank's message.

His companion was bringing the Uzi to bear on the Beretta's muzzle-flash. Mack Bolan stroked the weapon's hair trigger twice in rapid succession. The twin 9mm parabellum slugs covered the distance from muzzle to target hot on the trail of one another.

The first caught some portion of the Israeli-manufactured weapon. The slug's force drove the man backward as if he'd been punched.

The second jacketed bit of death located his coat button. With the brass button leading the way, the parabellum slug plowed its way into and through the breastbone. The heavy metal button acted as an expander, and the chunk of parabellum terror continued to do its deadly work. The corner of the guy's right lung area suddenly developed an inability to do its job. Fragments from the brass button tore a trio of rips in the muscle of the heart itself. That valiant organ continued to pump its life-giving fluid. Thimblefuls of precious crimson filled the chest cavity within the first second. A pair of beats later and enough blood to fill a man's cupped hand flowed into the damaged lung area.

His Uzi forgotten, the man dropped to the deck. It was as though some powerful but invisible hand descended from above to force his body to the wet planks.

"What's happening up there? What's going on?" the voice from the stern called apprehensively. Automatically the guy's hand moved the throttle up another notch, figuring it was better to reverse halfway back into the bay than run into trouble and hole the bow. Those blacktop cowboys up front were lucky to find their own butts in the dark and fog, let alone cast a line properly.

As the half-dead man frantically fought to suck air into his lungs, Bolan scrambled down the length of the pier. Uneven planking caught at his toes and threatened his balance.

Like some sleek, lithe killer cat out of the night, the Executioner dashed to the end of the pier. The faint glow of lighted controls told him where his prey was peering into the gloom.

At that moment the capricious breeze sucked long tendrils of fog into a dense cluster. The lighted control panel was instantly lost to view.

Bolan triggered a 9mm probe into the night. He was rewarded by the sound of breaking glass as the slug ripped into and through the Spartan wheelhouse. A second and third time the Beretta whispered its tale of death. Two more slugs tore through the walls of the craft's protective cabin. But the boat continued to move out into the bay.

IN THE CABIN, the hand that had held the throttle wide open was now clenched in sudden pain. Hot

metal tore its way through the helmsman's trousers
and into his left thigh. The slug's mate buried itself
harmlessly in the boat's ancient stern, inches from
the man's shoulder.

A pair of dull thuds caught the helmsman's attention as two more 9mm parabellums searched for flesh
and found seasoned oak instead.

The man knew he was hit. But the pain was more a
dull throbbing ache than searing hurt. He slowed the
laboring engine to the point where he could horse it
out of reverse. Without ever looking back at whatever had come out of the night fog, he set course
toward Eagle Nest Island.

Once the boat was going at full speed, he dropped
a knotted lashing onto the wheel. Then he gave his
complete attention to his wound.

With gentle and cautious fingers the guy probed
his injury. For a terrible second he thought he had
lost control of his bladder. But no, his crotch area
was too sticky for it to be urine. It was blood. Good
Christ, he was bleeding to death.

With fingers he could now barely control, he un-
hitched his belt. Shifting his weight to his good leg,
he eased blood-soaked trousers down to his knees.
Then he fumbled his lighter out of a pocket that was
now around his ankles.

In mounting panic he willed his hand to jerk the
lighter's wheel. On the third attempt the lighter gave
forth a flame that flickered and threatened to go out
in the breeze.

Oh, God, oh, God, no. The crimson mess of torn

tissue was his flesh. And his blood. It was spurting from the savaged tissue as if someone were behind it with a pump.

Think. What to do. Have to think. Think before you get fuzzy. Direct pressure. Raise the limb. Sterile compresses. Use a tourniquet only if willing to sacrifice the limb.

Pressure, that was the ticket. The spurting was lessening a bit, and he had not even started pressing on it. Maybe it just looked worse than it was. That was it. A flesh wound but not all that serious.

As he sought something to use as a compress, the hardguy tried to remember something important about wounds that spurted. Arteries or veins? Which one spurted?

He was tired. So damned tired. Just ease back against the hard seat and rest a minute or two. Eagle Nest Island was coming up quickly now. The old hulk was veering away from the landing, but it didn't matter. He would correct the wheel, which was lashed solidly, in just a minute. The worst that could happen would be the boat turning in a big circle.

The lighter fell forgotten at his feet. His eyes fluttered, then remained closed. By the time he remembered what he knew about the danger of severed arteries, it really made no difference. No difference at all.

ON THE ISLAND, Big Jim Lane wiped a light froth of beer from his lips with the back of his huge hand. Jesse Lobato and some punk whose name Lane could not recall sat glued to the portable TV set across from him.

Big Jim grunted and drained the remainder of the can in a single swallow. Without effort he crushed the can in his massive right paw, then looked around the room that served as a combination day room and communications center.

This island gig came about as close to a prison term as any contract he had ever taken. Eagle Nest or bat den or whatever the hell the godforsaken chunk of rock and trees was called, was enough to drive him stark raving nuts. Getting the docks and boathouse and other structures built was a pain. Having to live in them was an even bigger pain.

And those stinking fishing boats. Enough to gag a maggot. And if the smell didn't kill you, then the bobbing and bouncing in the ocean would. What a mess. Import-export was fine—but not up here, buried in the exposed armpit of New England.

Big Jim Lane considered himself number one in his business. And the business of supplying terrorists and street fighters with military hardware had never been better. It was about as hard as snapping his thick fingers for Big Jim to have the boys hit a National Guard armory or Army reserve depot and pick up enough weaponry to restart the Civil War. Or, if foreign stuff was needed, a couple of phone calls, a cable or two, and one of Big Jim's boats would meet a freighter out at sea. It was that easy once you had your organization set up and running smoothly.

But this! He snapped the ring on another can of

beer and gulped most of its contents in a long swig. This was something else again. The only boats worth setting foot on were those his boys ran up from Boston. And they were sitting idle in the new boathouse.

He could understand the wisdom in using local fishing and lobstering craft to make off-shore pickups and deliveries. It made sense. Not that the exchanges were difficult. They were not. People were a lot easier and quicker to move than guns. Men could scramble up and down rope ladders. At least these guys could. Big Jim gulped the remainder of the can, then crushed it.

Moving these guys in and out of the country was kids' play. But sitting here and watching that goddamn fog come in and bury you was the pits. And the people who ran those stinking old wooden tubs... they were like characters out of the movies. He shook his massive head.

It was his first gig in Maine. Big Jim fervently hoped it would be his last. The locals who lived around the bay gave him the creeps, the absolute skin-crawling willies. They never smiled. Most of the time they never talked. They just looked at a guy and right through him. It was their hard eyes that made a man afraid to turn his back.

Big Jim reached for another beer. The hell with them. They were so badly panicked they would certainly not give Jim and his boys any trouble. They had turned in their weapons. They were moving people back and forth like a flock of good little sheep. That was one thing Big Jim could guarantee. Once his boys showed people it was to their advantage to cooperate, they cooperated.

"Jesse." Big Jim raised his voice to carry over the sound from the TV. "Any word yet about Hank?" He knew there was not. Hell, there couldn't have been, or Jim would have heard the radio from where he sat.

"Not yet, boss. Manny and a couple of troops are checking it out." Jesse never took his eyes from the set.

"Well, check on it from time to time. We got important cargo due in later tonight. There can't be any slipups on this shipment, or some of you guys will have to learn to walk while carrying your head."

"Right, boss. Everything's under control. Where's this bunch from? Libya?"

"Who knows? Or cares for that matter."

The door to the communications room opened to admit Bad Louie Stevens and Murph O'Reilly. Streamers of fog trailed behind them, only to be cut off by the door's closing.

"Any word from Manny?" Murph demanded.

"Not yet."

"That fog's the worst it's been all week," Bad Louie complained. "Can't see more than five, maybe ten feet."

"Murph." Big Jim suddenly made a decision. "I hate like hell to have you do it, but roust some of the guys out and post double security. I've got bad vibes about tonight. And we can't have anything go wrong tonight. Not tonight of all nights."

Murph stubbed out his cigarette and turned to do Big Jim's bidding. Bad Louie's eyes met those of the huge man whose orders he accepted without question.

"You think we overlooked something?"

Big Jim shook his head and sipped more beer. "Nah. It's just the fog and this damned island and those blasted people ashore...."

6

Mack Bolan made certain the car that was creeping through the fog was his. Then he broke cover and moved toward the vehicle. The kid must be used to driving in this pea-soup fog.

Rick toed the brake the instant Bolan's blackclad form edged into the car's low beam.

"Sorry it took me so long, Mr. Phoenix. Fog's really settling in. Looks as though it's here for the night, or at least for most of it."

"Do you think it'll lift later?"

Rick Cartright seemed to sniff the air before answering. "I can't say for sure. Sometimes it lifts about one or two in the morning. The land begins to cool down by then."

"Let's get that trunk open."

The youth left the driver's seat to join Bolan at the back of the car. When the trunk light illuminated the cargo area, Bolan heard the kid's quick intake of breath.

"Is that a Thompson submachine gun?" the boy asked in an awe-filled voice.

"It's an M-3. This one was manufactured about the time of World War II. It's slow-firing. Only about four hundred rounds per minute. But it's got a modified barrel and bolt so it can handle 9mm parabellum rounds.''

''Wouldn't it have to have a new magazine as well?''

Bolan let his eyes cut over toward the kid. ''It's got an adapter.'' The kid was well informed, even if he didn't know an M-3 from a Thompson. ''This model has a flash hider. That's another reason I chose it.''

Rick nodded his understanding.

At Bolan's request the young man handed him a web belt from which a pair of fragmentation grenades hung ready. Rick's eyes widened again, but he made no comment. In silence the wiry youth watched as John Phoenix divided his supply of plastic explosives for easy packing. Half a dozen radio-controlled detonators and their remote unit topped off the big warrior's gear.

''Is that the stuff they call goop?'' Rick asked.

''Some do. Plastic is a good enough term.''

''How about plastique?''

''That's fine, too. You read a lot, don't you?''

''Does it show?''

''A bit. Keep it up.''

''And now you need a boat.''

Yeah, the kid was no dummy.

''They took Uncle Ed's after they....'' His voice suddenly cracked. ''After they killed him.'' The words were forced past tightly drawn lips.

''And Becky's grandfather has been out most of

the day. We couldn't use his trawler anyhow. But I think his dory is still tied up at the dock. I know we can use it. I'll row you across.''

Together they started out on foot in the direction of the village lights.

''Is Becky's grandfather out fishing?''

''No way. He left old Bill Welch behind. Bill's crewed for Tom Devereaux for as long as I can remember. Tom went out alone today.''

''Is that usual?''

''The way things have been going around here for the last month or so, who knows what's usual or not?''

''Any ideas?''

''My guess is he's either meeting a ship at sea or he went down to Boston for cargo.''

''Illegal cargo?''

''If it was legal he'd have taken Bill Welch with him.'' The kid's clipped tone indicated he'd said all he intended to. They walked on in silence.

In the near distance a dog, alerted by the sound of their approach, started an insistent barking. Rick spoke its name, and the animal fell silent.

They passed two lighted dwellings before Rick turned off the path toward a third. Still in the lead, the kid stepped onto the wooden porch. He stamped his deck shoes on the wood several times as though to clean them of any mud or dirt.

Bolan recognized the gesture for what it was: an informal announcement of their presence. Rick's knuckles beat a quick, light message on the doorframe. When the knocking brought no response, Rick repeated it.

Footfalls approached the door from inside. A latch clicked, and the door opened to allow a sliver of yellow light to intrude into the night.

"It's Rick Cartright, Mrs. Devereaux. I've got a friend with me. His name is Mr. John Phoenix. May we come in for a minute?"

The door swung fractionally wider to admit Rick's slim body. Bolan was forced to push gently against the wooden door to enter the room.

For a minute the big guy in battle black silently faced the middle-aged woman as they measured each other. Everything about her seemed to be sharp angles, and her lined face showed the weariness of years of New England survival. Tall, thin, almost bony, Mrs. Devereaux was a living caricature of the sea- and weather-battered dwellers who made their living from the waters of coastal Maine.

She gave no indication of what she thought of the man in black. Her sharp blue eyes took in his every feature without any change in expression.

"And this is Becky's great-aunt, Mrs. Whitmore." Rick broke the room's stillness with his introduction.

Bolan turned his attention to the other woman whose presence he noted when he entered the tidy room.

The women were two of a kind, though Mrs. Whitmore appeared a few years younger than Becky's grandmother. She did not greet Bolan, but stood somewhat stiffly in the corner of the room. An unspoken signal passed between the two women. Mrs. Whitmore moved toward the room's center. Behind her lay a butcher knife whose fifteen-inch blade glinted brightly on the top of an ancient china hutch.

"You fixin' to start a war?" Mrs. Devereaux's voice was strangely full and rich, not at all in keeping with her bony limbs and jutting elbows.

"If I have to," Bolan told her.

His answer satisfied her. She turned her back on the big guy. "Velma, why don't you set two more places for Rick and Mr. Phoenix." To Bolan she said, "My sister and I were just going to have a cup of tea. You'll join us, won't you?"

Time was in short supply for Mack Bolan. Yet he understood the invitation was a form of welcome, of acceptance.

"We're a bit pressed for time, but we'd be happy to. Thank you."

She nodded, then led the way toward the kitchen. Four cups and saucers now adorned a spotless linen tablecloth spread on the kitchen table.

"We came by the pigpen," Rick said. "The pigs were hungry, so I fed them some cracked corn. It's not near enough to satisfy them, but I thought I'd better not give them any more. They sounded like they hadn't been fed all day. Maybe not since yesterday."

"Thank you, Rick. I'll see they get fed properly."

Her tone belied her words. The woman had more on her mind than the hungry sows.

"How long will Becky be up at Bangor?" Rick accepted a homemade cookie to accompany his cup of tea.

"Not long, I reckon." The eyes of the two sisters met again in a quick flash that was not lost on Bolan.

"You said she's at her aunt's," Rick continued. He didn't look up from the table when he spoke.

"I seem to recall telling you that."

Her wording caught Bolan's trained ear. She did not tell Rick that Becky was there, only admitted having told him she was.

"Maybe I might just call her on the phone." Rick's words were casual, his face guileless.

"Don't do that," Mrs. Devereaux said too quickly, staring at the youth until he raised his eyes to meet hers. "It won't do you any good, Rick. And it might do Becky harm."

This time the eyes that locked belonged to Bolan and the kid. In uneasy silence, the quartet sipped the scalding tea.

"Mrs. Devereaux, I'd like to borrow your husband's dory if I may." Rick came to the point of their visit.

"Going fishing in this fog?"

Bolan grinned inwardly. He liked her style.

Rick hesitated, then received permission from Bolan's all but imperceptible lifting of dark brows.

"I'm going to row Mr. Phoenix out to the island."

"The tide's coming in. Mind those submerged rocks just off the near end. Reckon you don't want to hole the boat and have to swim back."

"Thanks, Mrs. Devereaux. I'll take care."

Rick looked at Bolan, then turned back to Mrs. Devereaux. "We'd best be getting on our way, Mrs. Devereaux," the boy said. "Thanks for the tea and cookies."

"Thank you very much, ladies." Bolan pushed back the straight wooden chair and came to his feet.

"If you're thinking of landing on the island and moving around a bit, you won't go far dressed like that," Mrs. Devereaux said to Bolan, getting to her feet. "Let me get you some of Tom's gear. You can slip it on right over that outfit you're wearing."

Without waiting for his response she left the room and moved toward an enclosed rear porch. Seconds later she returned with stained trousers and a dark waterproof jacket. A black knitted cap and worn rubber-soled boots completed the fisherman's outfit.

"Thank you," Bolan said as he accepted the offering. All but the clumsy boots were welcome in the event he had to blend in and mingle with the troops on the island.

Bolan and Rick were already at the door when Mrs. Devereaux said, "There's one more thing." She addressed her words directly to Rick.

"You remember that foreign-sounding man in the shiny black shoes? The one who frightened Mrs. Barlow so badly a week ago tomorrow?"

"Do you mean the man who asked her how much she'd miss her baby if he burned up in a fire?"

"That's him. He's been standing guard down at

the dock. Been there since noon. Won't let anyone out onto the pier.''

Her steely blue eyes took in Bolan's weaponry.

"Some men are just too ornery mean to be allowed to live.''

With that, she opened the door in silent invitation.

When they were well clear of the modest house and moving downslope toward the incoming tide, Rick spoke.

"Becky is a lot like her grandmother. She's pretty, sure. Actually beautiful. But inside she's got that same toughness.''

"She must be quite a girl.''

"She is.'' Then in fairness he added, "And so is Mrs. Devereaux. And her sister. They're worried sick about Becky. I can tell. I just know she's on the island! Why else would Tom take his trawler out alone? They've taken Becky and are holding her to make sure he does what they want!''

Bolan could find no fault with Rick's logic. Silently he thrust the bundle of clothing into Rick's arms. With a touch of his hand he indicated that he wanted the kid to shorten stride and remain behind him. They were approaching the pier.

"Give me sixty seconds,'' Bolan ordered, his voice low. "Then start kicking some rocks around and make enough noise to attract his attention. Stay low just in case he gets jumpy.''

Without pausing for the kid's response, Bolan melted into the darkness of early night. The constant noise of the sea lapping at the ancient dock covered any sound the big guy might make. But it did more than that. It also obscured any noise the man on guard might make. It was a toss-up Bolan accepted.

Keeping low, becoming black on black, he moved forward. With every sense alert, his hand wrapped around the eager Beretta, he moved ahead.

The breeze pushed the smell of his prey's cigarette to him even before Bolan sighted the red glow through the misty fog. The acrid smoke was sharp and out of place amid the smell of fish long dead and the sea's ever-present and distinctive odor.

Bolan moved close enough to study the outline of the unsuspecting guard. The man wore a city hat, nylon windbreaker, and a pair of twill trousers that must have come from L.L. Bean down in Freeport. The guy probably imagined the Bean pants automatically made him one of the locals.

Going native wouldn't be a concern for much longer, however.

The Beretta spit flame twice, the first slug shattering a portion of the man's lower jaw. The second 9mm flesh-mangler entered the man's chest. Inside his chest the guy's heart tried to figure how to cope with major damage. It failed.

The kid was at Bolan's side almost instantly.

Rick peered into the dark but made no attempt to get out his flashlight.

"That's two down. At least two of the bastards won't be threatening to burn little babies alive," the kid said.

Yeah. Rick did not know about the two, maybe

three in the diesel-powered craft. And it was just as well. Some things went better unknown and unsaid.

"Let's get that dory into the water," Bolan said. "Somewhere out there a young lady is depending on us."

7

Big Jim Lane was aware of the commotion long before Murph reentered the day room.

"Boss, I think you'd better come down to the landing. We've got problems. Big problems."

Big Jim was on his feet and moving toward the door.

"What's happening?"

Murph dogged his boss's steps like the faithful cur he was. "One of the guys heard this diesel coming in the fog, running full-out. Only the sound kept coming and then going. He finally figured out it was running in circles. That guy Stiles from the village went out with a couple of the guys and slipped up beside the boat.

"It was Manny's—the one he took in to check on Hank."

"And?" Getting Murph to come to the point could be almost like pulling molars.

"The wheel was lashed, and that was what was taking the tub around and around. Manny was dead at the helm. The two troops with him were both dead up in the bow. The boat looks like the kill floor of a packing plant."

"What about Hank?"

"No sign of him, boss. Just the three."

Big Jim's ear caught the slight change in the noise made by the one big generator currently on line. The area just ahead brightened as portable high-intensity lights were switched on. Despite the fog, the area became bright. It was now more like a bar full of smoke than the inside of a coffin.

Characteristically, Stiles stood apart from the gaping troops. In spite of the fact that the lean seaman was part of the local scene, Big Jim liked the man. No, strike that. Admired the independent cuss. Stiles knew his boat and he knew the sea. And he knew that if he didn't perform and deliver for as long as Big Jim Lane needed him, he'd sail home to find his wife and three kids cut into fish bait.

"It's the boss."

"Stand clear. Let Big Jim have a look."

Underlings stood aside as their big leader moved forward. Once able to view the trio of bloody corpses laid out on the newly built floating dock, Big Jim wished he had taken Murph's word for it.

Out of all the carnage it was Manny's face, ghostly pale in the lights' harsh glare, that drew and held his attention.

"Why is he so white?" Lane demanded of no one, of anyone.

"Just about all his blood's gone," a hushed voice informed the giant of a man. "A bullet just tore the living hell out of his thigh."

"Any idea who did this?"

A broken chorus of scattered denials came instantly.

"How about you?" Big Jim fixed Stiles with a direct glare as though to impale the Maine resident with his gaze.

"No one from Kenlandport did that." His flat tone lost none of its characteristic twang despite the emotion of the moment.

"You'd better be sure of that. Damned sure."

"I'm sure."

Damn. First that Warner character broke free of his fear and tried to call in outside help. Now this. And if there was a time Big Jim didn't need any more worries, it was now. Not with major cargo due soon.

"Wrap them up in canvas or something. Get them off the dock. Put the bodies somewhere out of sight. Murph."

"Right here, boss."

"Check that security. Mount a captain of the guard. Until I tell you different, this site has just gone hard."

"Got it." O'Reilly moved instantly to do Big Jim's bidding.

Bad Louie Stevens was at his side though Big Jim had no recollection of the smaller man's arrival. The two moved away from the immediate area.

"Some of you guys get that boat cleaned up. We may need it later." Big Jim's command was directed to the silent group as a whole.

When no one moved, Lane's voice became a bellow. "Get your asses in gear, dammit! You—Stiles. Choose two soldiers and get going."

Without waiting to see his orders carried out, the big man lumbered back in the direction from which he came. In his wake Bad Louie trailed like a skiff towed by a tug.

"Do you think the enemy is near?" Bad Louie ventured after checking to make certain his words would reach only the ears of his leader.

"I don't know what to think. I know for sure I don't like what's happening. And for damned sure I don't like this fog."

"It gets to me, too, boss."

When the pair burst into the day room, Big Jim directed his first words to Jesse Lobato, whose interest was still centered on the small television screen.

"Any word from Hank?"

"Nothing yet, boss." Jesse didn't look away from the image on the screen.

Big Jim's voice was deceptively calm. "Lobato, how'd you like to wear that set?"

The troop's head came up instantly.

"Sorry, boss." He nudged the guy at his side. "Turn that thing off, Fish."

"You guys better get down to the dock and get useful." Bad Louie signaled them from the room with a wagging of his bushy brows. "Manny just bought it."

The pair fled the scene.

Bad Louie popped a pair of tabs and extended one of the cold cans toward Big Jim. The can disappeared within Lane's huge hairy paw.

"So what about this stranger?" Bad Louie asked when the silence threatened to stretch.

"All I can say for sure is if I get my hands on him, I'll turn him into something that'll make that Warner guy look like we took him to a Sunday-school picnic."

Bad Louie pulled at the cold brew and nodded his agreement. When Big Jim said something, he meant it. Louie only hoped he could help work over that snooping newcomer. He had missed out on Ed Warner. From what Louie heard, it was one hell of a party.

WHILE RICK MANEUVERED the heavy old dory into the lapping waves, Bolan shouldered the body of the guard. It took only seconds to slip the dead man out of sight beneath an overturned dory on the dock. The chances of a change of guard were good. When the relief was unable to locate the guy on duty, it would create added confusion. And as both strategist and tactician, Mack Bolan knew only too well the value of confusion as a weapon.

The Executioner added the borrowed clothing to the litter of sacking, canvas and odds and ends already in the rowboat. With a quick extension of leg, back and shoulder muscles, he launched the dory. The kid drew back on the long, clumsy oars a few strokes. He turned the craft on its own axis without obvious effort, bow now pointing forward. Then the deceptively lean youth began to put his entire body into each stroke of the oars.

Despite the fact that Rick Cartright obviously knew how to handle the chore he had set for himself, progress against the incoming tide was slow. And having once cleared the shelter afforded the bobbing dory by the small bay, the water roughened. Though by no means a heavily running sea, the incoming waves were still sufficient to turn the voyage into a carnival ride.

The kid rowed without speaking. From time to time he glanced over his shoulder in an effort to orient himself in the foggy night. Steadily, with no signs of faltering, Rick moved the dory through the choppy night water. It wasn't all that long before Bolan was able to make out the shadowy outline of the island crouched on the dark horizon.

Every so often patches of open air were formed by the eddying breeze.

"Fog's going to clear later." The teenager at the oars was breathing easily despite his efforts.

That could become a mixed blessing, Bolan realized. Since it was beyond his control, he chose to neither wish for nor dread the possibility.

Several times phrases and bits of conversation were carried across the water from the island's south side. Once the dory passed the rocky end of tree-covered island, the bits and pieces of speech came to them no more.

Some four hundred yards along the island's north side, Rick began edging the craft toward the waiting chunk of rock and trees.

When Rick spoke his voice was pitched low. "I'm going to try to run ashore here. I'll head in just to the right of some big boulders that jut out into the water. That's your right, I mean."

Bolan peered ahead. Vague shapes of dark, silent danger crouched in menace. A curtain of fog rolled in and the huge boulders vanished like a bad dream. The sound of wave-lap on the rocky shore was all that remained.

When Rick dug in an oar, the heavy dory used it as a pivot point. Bolan felt cold spray as a wave broke over the boat's blunt stern. Rick reacted to the frigid water with a muffled grunt.

"There's a stiff current running. I'm going to need all the help you can provide once we get in close. Be ready to jump out when I give you the word. But watch your footing. It's all rocky beach."

Now the dory was in the grip of the current. The bow rose, only to slam down hard. Bolan gripped the hull with both hands. No, he was not afraid of water. But any person who ignored the powerful threat of the angry water was a fool.

For a passing instant it seemed that Rick had lost control. The dory's clumsy stern threatened to come around. One oar flashed silver as its blade came free of the angry sea.

Then the craft steadied. Bolan knew Rick was putting every ounce of his waning strength into the heavy oars. The kid was trying desperately to back-paddle. His attempt to slow their approach was like trying to stop a charging bull.

The incoming waves became erratic convolutions beneath the dory's ancient hull. A jutting hunk of rock flashed past on the starboard side. It was there and gone before Bolan saw it through the dense fog.

They passed so close that the Executioner could have touched it with his hand.

And in that instant disaster struck. Rick had sensed the upcoming boulder. But not in time, due to his concentration on the bucking, jolting dory.

He had the starboard oar almost clear before the protruding chunk of danger smashed it from his grasp. The oar jerked free. Its oarlock kept it from going overboard, but there was no way Rick could retrieve it in time to regain control.

"Lost an oar!"

Bolan heard no panic in the kid's words.

The dory twisted like an anguished sea creature in its death throes. For a bad instant, the boat threatened to broach.

Instinctively, Bolan threw his weight against the uplifting side of the hull. The move was enough to make the difference.

The dory settled back into the frantic current.

The boulders Rick was steering for loomed out of the dark. The kid had called them big. But in truth they were huge. Their towering bulk made the dory and its occupants tiny by comparison.

Rick's weight shift drew Mack's attention. He snapped his eyes from the rocky shore ahead. He sensed immediately what the kid was trying to do. He turned and lunged for the oarlock. It came free when he pried it from its housing.

"Got it!" Rick's voice held triumph.

The youth grasped the thick shaft in both hands. Then he thrust it over the stern. The single oar now became a rudder. If Rick could manage to hold on to it, he might even use the oar to scull with.

Just as Bolan again faced the onrushing shore, the dory's bow rose. The wooden hull yawed toward port. The crunch and scrape of rock on vessel was a deadly sound.

Rick was a dark shape sailing over Bolan's shoulder. The night warrior grabbed for the kid. Grabbed and missed. He vanished into the churning froth of the waves. The heavy oar followed him into the sea. The blade of the airborne oar caught Bolan a glancing blow back of the ear. By then it was the least of his worries. He, too, was in the cold grasp of the roiling waters.

Bolan hit bottom and drove upward with all his strength. He surfaced just as the dory slid free of its imprisoning rock. Man and boat collided. Momentarily stunned, Mack grabbed at the hull and hung on.

From the corner of his eye he saw something dark break the water's rough surface. It was Rick's head. Eel slick, his hair formed a black helmet. Bolan saw the youth grab a lungful of air. Then he had his own worries.

There was no clear direction in the current. The placement of jutting rocks caused the waves to form chaotic patterns. Concealed boulders altered those patterns. There was no logic to the waters.

The dory was coming around, using Bolan as a crude sea anchor. Before he was able to avoid it, the craft was between him and the sea. The rocky seabed grabbed at his feet and threatened to trip him up. The relentless push of waves against dory drove both man and boat ashore.

Rick yelled something at him. The words became a sound without meaning.

And suddenly Bolan was pinned against an immovable jutting of stone. The dory was a fantastic force pressing against him.

With all the strength available to his arms and shoulders, Mack Bolan tried to fend off the wooden monster. Rather than push uselessly outward, he sought to twist the craft to one side. For too many lost beats, Bolan knew he had failed. The life was being crushed from him. Strong though he was, he was physically unable to expand his lungs.

Slowly the dory began to respond. Slowly at first, then with increasing speed, it sideslipped away. Bolan let the craft go free, preoccupied for the moment in drawing air into tortured lungs. The dory reached shore with a scrape of wood on stone. Then it began to withdraw.

Bolan gained his balance in the swirling water and lunged for the dory. Suddenly docile, it allowed him to shove it ashore, well above the clutching fingers of the icy water.

Water droplets flashed as the capricious breeze momentarily thinned the fog. Rick was using a single overhand stroke to come toward shore. In his other hand he clutched the oar that had followed him overboard.

Bolan glanced at the dory. The second oar was still secure in its lock.

He helped Rick stumble through the last half-dozen feet of rocks and water. The kid placed the oar silently in the dory. Then he collapsed to sit on the hard discomfort of the stony beach. Bolan knelt beside him.

Rick drew half a dozen long, sobbing breaths. Bolan placed a hand on the kid's shoulder. Beneath sodden material, muscles jerked and danced in the rhythm of exhaustion.

Rick looked up, met Bolan's gaze.

"Sorry. I screwed up.

"Don't worry. We made it."

"Suppose anyone heard us? There was a hell of a noise when that rock damn near holed the dory. And then I yelled my fool head off."

"We'll just sit here and give it a couple of minutes."

Mack's nylon suit had protected him somewhat from the icy cold of the seawater; it allowed a thin film of liquid to coat his body beneath the garment and prevent the kind of severe heat-loss that Rick had experienced.

Sooner than Mack dared hope, the youth's muscle twitches slowed and all but ceased. Rick raised his head and peered about in the off-and-on fog.

"At least we're exactly where I thought we were." It was a small triumph.

Meanwhile Bolan completed checking himself and the dory. Nothing was missing despite their nearly disastrous landing.

"Do you want to use the clothing Mrs. Devereaux gave you?" The boy's lips were close to the big guy's ear.

"Not this trip. I'm going to do a quick reconnaissance from this side. Depending on what I discover I'll either cross the island or have you row me around to the landing area. In that case I'll go with the clothing."

"Let's go."

Bolan recognized and understood the kid's need to be a part of the operation. He also realized the danger of what needed doing. And at the same time the man known as Colonel John Phoenix was aware the youth at his side was not one to be put off by explanations of danger. Instantly he reached a compromise.

Bolan gave Rick quick instructions. "Let's move inland about ten paces. I want you to take up observation there. Protect my back while I do a quick recon. If you spot anyone, heave a rock into the woods toward me. Just throw the rock and get down."

Bolan felt the kid's dissatisfaction with the order. At the same time he sensed the boy would carry it out. Together they moved forward.

Though less dense than on the mainland, the undergrowth still hindered their advance and made silence doubly difficult to maintain. Twice the kid stooped to retrieve rocks from the forest floor.

When Bolan pulled to a halt beside a thick-trunked tree, the kid was at his side as close as his own shadow. He indicated the tree with a jerk of his hand, and the kid nodded and stood fast.

Alone, Bolan moved more rapidly through the

dark woods. Much as he might have liked to scout the area in a crisscross fashion, Bolan opted for a quick forward movement. He desperately needed to get a firsthand look at his eventual goal.

When he viewed the lighted landing area from the raised spine of the narrow island, Bolan's trained eye quickly took in the tightly grouped buildings. In the harsh glare of the high-intensity lights, the area had a somewhat unearthly look about it in the fog. The combination of the bright lights and a rising breeze enabled the Executioner to study the site sufficiently to commit the layout to memory. Boathouse, generator building, mess and sleeping facilities, and command area all formed a compact site.

Movement from the dock caught his attention. Men in pairs strained to move canvas-wrapped bundles toward the shore. Bolan allowed himself a passing feeling of satisfaction. The troops removing the three bodies would keep the bloodied remains in mind for hours to come. Along with confusion, apprehension was an effective battlefield strategy.

Certain now that he needed to move among them, Bolan prepared to retreat from his forward observation post. Rapid movement caught and held his gaze. Armed men were being dispatched toward the site's perimeter. They moved at the double and seemed to have a clear idea of what was expected of them.

Bolan smiled inwardly. Exactly what any good field commander would do. Double or even triple the strength on the outposts. Protect against enemy advance. Defend the hardsite.

The increased number of troops assigned to beef up the perimeter meant that he would have to deal with fewer men when he hit the site. And hit it he would. Only Mack Bolan planned to come in from the sea. That was the one direction from which an attack was not expected. Therefore it was the one direction from which The Executioner would come.

As though the elements had determined that the warrior in night garb needed no further time for observation, the breeze died. Tendrils of fog again began to seek out the forest floor, but it didn't matter. Bolan was already moving toward the waiting kid.

Bolan made few mistakes in his life. He could not afford them and continue to survive. But in the darkened woods on Eagle Nest Island the guy in black made an error. As combat errors go it was not major. But in Bolan's trade any mistake could instantly amplify and become life-threatening.

His quick recon told Bolan the troops were city-born and -bred. Only the lean, silent man in the drab and worn gear of a working boat handler seemed local. Once having determined the adversary to be from the streets and alleys of urban jungles, Bolan dismissed their ability once away from familiar turf.

Moving rapidly and in near total silence, he made his way back toward the waiting Rick Cartright. Secure in the knowledge that he would detect anything foreign to the scene, Bolan was already planning the probe he intended to make.

The sentry rose out of the dark like a silent shadow of death. Only Bolan's superb reflexes enabled him to get an arm up in time to keep the wide-swinging blow from taking off the top of his head. Ducking, twisting, Bolan was falling away from the swinging weapon when contact came. The blow's effectiveness was diminished by the fact Bolan was moving away at the time of impact. Even so, the force of the round-house swing of the club instantly took all feeling and use from his left arm.

Too late to try for the Beretta, too late to go for a groin kick, Bolan deliberately let the club drive him back. Using the attacker's force to give speed to his own move, Bolan rolled clear. He put valuable distance between himself and the big goon who materialized from nowhere.

In the space of a single heartbeat Bolan recognized his adversary. Not as an individual but as a type. It was in that instant Mack Bolan realized his mental error.

Not all members of the criminal element who prowl city streets in search of prey are city dwellers by accident of birth. Some come to the city to escape the twin evils of rural poverty and a life of unrewarded effort. This was one of them. At a guess Bolan placed his point of origin as a wooded mountain area in West Virginia, Kentucky, or Tennessee.

Like so many, the guy gravitated north and east to become another violent predator in the asphalt jungle. Whether the migration was prefaced by a tour in Vietnam was a moot question at this point. What was important was that the man was strong, had the advantage for the moment, and enjoyed inflicting pain and suffering. Had it been otherwise, he'd have simply blown Bolan to hell with either his side arm or his primary piece. The use of the club indicated a desire to maim as a portion of the death rite.

Off balance, still in backward motion, Bolan struggled to get his powerful legs under him. The guy was on him like a big hungry forest creature lusting for fresh meat. The straight length of oak probed for Bolan as the man closed the distance separating them in a bound.

The end of the club smashed into Bolan's breastbone, driving him back and toward the earth. A painful, numbing tingle spread outward from the point of impact. And in that instant Bolan knew.

The use of the end of the club, the blow to the breastbone, indicated police training. Yeah, the guy was the product of a military police unit somewhere. Probably took part in riot training. Maybe even helped keep some sort of order during those last chaotic days of the final American withdrawal from that Southeast Asian hell.

A tree trunk halted Mack Bolan's backward movement. Instinctively he drew his legs toward him ready to lash out with both feet. And just as instinctively the attacker moved to his own left to avoid the direct impact of those feet. It was Bolan's first break and the only one he needed.

Instead of trying to swivel to keep his feet toward the guy with the club, Bolan filled his fist with the Beretta's comforting weight. Three times the gun whispered in rapid succession. And each whisper was accompanied by the departure of a 9mm flesh-tearing jacketed slug. As though to light their way, the muzzle flashed with each muffled report.

The guy could have survived the first hit. The slug struck a rib a glancing blow, altered its direction, and plowed its path through muscle and tissue. It exited just below the left collarbone.

The second did even less permanent damage. It caught the edge of the club and became a misshapen ricochet. The torn and twisted chunk of metal ripped flesh and tissue from just below the man's rib cage. It was a painful wound, though far from fatal.

It was the third of the trio of 9mm rippers that actually did the job. The slug entered the guy's throat, impacted with the delicate structure of the larynx and exited from the back of the muscular neck. On its way out of the still-living body, the metallic messenger of death took with it a piece of cervical vertebrae. That severed the spinal cord. The sentry who enjoyed administering physical pain died while still on his feet.

Bolan returned the Beretta to its holster and stood up. Despite the numbness, his left fingers flexed slowly at his urging. The arm would return to usefulness shortly.

The sound of a crackling branch came to him from the near distance. Like a shadow fading among its fellows, Bolan blended with a tree trunk. Beretta once more in hand, he waited.

The slim figure was less than five yards from where Bolan waited when the big guy made absolutely positive identification.

"Rick." He hissed the single word into the night.

The kid halted instantly, head up, totally alert.

Bolan showed himself and again returned gun to leathered safety. "I told you to hold your position."

"I heard sounds and figured you needed help," the youth said, defending his action. At that instant Rick caught sight of the fallen sentry. He peered into the gloom in an effort to study the man.

"That's three less for us to worry about," the kid said. "Now what?"

"Back to the dory. Let's row around the east end of the island and pay our friends a visit."

The pair moved rapidly toward their waiting craft.

"You mean just row up to their dock?"

"It's the best way I know of to check them out up close. It wouldn't surprise me a bit if they might be in need of a replacement."

"Or two."

Together they muscled the heavy dory afloat. Bolan helped push it effortlessly into the sea despite the diminished strength in his left arm.

The kid was again straining at the long oars when he told Bolan, "I meant what I said. I'm coming with you. All the way."

Bolan made no reply. He understood the kid's need.

"Uncle Ed was about the closest thing I had to a family. I owe him."

Yeah, it was just as cut-and-dried as that. A kid no more than eighteen who could not weigh more than one hundred forty with his shoes full of salt water, turns his grief into action. And a search for justice. He is without family. His uncle has just been turned into the worst kind of turkey. His girl is probably kidnapped. Yet the kid rows a heavy dory without complaining and accepts everything as it comes.

Add to that the fact he is willing to follow Bolan's lead and walk right into the middle of a nest of vipers. All this with a single-bladed clasp knife in the right-hand pocket of his jeans.

From time to time the Executioner considered the futility of what he did and tried to do for a world incapable or unwilling to do for itself. Considered and came close to concluding his efforts were questionable at best.

And then along comes a Rick Cartright. And by his coming erases all doubt as to the rightness of what Mack Bolan did.

And, yeah, Bolan would continue to mentally refer to him as the kid. But the kid who pulled steadily at the oars was a man in every sense of the word. This was no kid brother; Bolan trusted that Rick Cartwright would take absolute responsibility for himself in a battle zone.

Feeling as suddenly refreshed as though just awakened from a long and pleasant sleep, the warrior in battle black peered ahead. The lighted landing area was now visible around the rocky point of the island.

8

While still well clear of the new dock, Mack Bolan slid into the seaman's gear except for the rubber boots. Those he left in full view of any who might look into the vessel. He stuffed his M-3, extra ammo, explosives and web belt with its dangling grenades beneath the sacking and canvas that lay at the bottom of the dory. It was not all that he might have wished for as far as hiding places go, but it was the best he could do under the circumstances.

With reluctance he unstrapped the .44 AutoMag and slid it out of sight under his seat. The Beretta remained in its holster beneath his left arm. In the bulky jacket he now wore, the outline of gunleather was impossible to spot.

A few yards out from the dock Bolan raised his voice.

"Hello there on the dock. We're coming in."

His words were the first clue most of those ashore had as to the boat's presence. Even the rhythmic creak of the oars in their locks had not alerted them. There was one exception, Bolan noted. The lean man in seaman's garb was conscious of their approach. Bolan realized the man was following their progress with his ears well before his keen eyes verified what he heard.

With every other stroke the kid was turning to peer quickly toward shore.

"Don't look into those lights," Bolan warned.

In the perimeter of the brightened area Bolan saw the kid's face clearly. A quick down-twist of lips told him his caution was unnecessary.

After another backward glance Rick muttered for only Bolan to hear, "The guy just standing there watching us. The skinny one. That's Bud Stiles."

"Friend?"

"He's from Kenlandport. He's got a wife and kids. Little kids. And just like the rest, Bud's scared bad."

The kid's reply was not a direct answer to Bolan's question. Even so, the meaning was clear.

Bolan shot a glance at his wrist. Only minutes past ten. Time pressure wasn't a major factor. Not yet, at least.

With casual skill born of long practice, the kid shipped the dockside oar and slid the heavy dory alongside the structure's fresh, raw wood.

Bolan slipped a line around a cleat and drew the stern in close. Stiles did the same at the bow while the kid brought the second oar aboard.

"Hi, Mr. Stiles." Rick's tone was bright, upbeat.

The thin man responded with a nod so slight Bolan would have missed it had he not been watching the fisherman with his peripheral vision. For his own part, Bud Stiles gave the big man his total attention. He made no effort to disguise or mask his scrutiny.

Bolan and the kid bounded easily onto the low dock.

"Bud. I'm Maurice Cherboneau. From up north of Rockland. You and I met a few years back when I was down talking with Tom Devereaux." Bolan hoped his "down East" twang was convincing.

It was obvious Stiles did not recall the meeting. It was equally apparent that Bolan's tactic was correct—and his accent accurate. Not only did the man relax, but several hard types standing nearby lost interest in the new arrivals. As far as they were concerned, Stiles had identified the pair in the boat. That was all that was necessary. They had more worrisome thoughts on their minds.

It was role camouflage of the most precarious order. But it was the best Bolan could do, so he rode with what he had.

He raised his voice and let his words carry. "I heard there might be some work available out here. Finance company took my boat last week. I'm about tapped out. Truth is I need a job and bad."

"Same goes for me." Rick took his cue and deliberately amplified his words. "I thought I had enough money to buy the stuff I need to finish that house I'm building. I thought wrong."

A broad man of medium height detached himself from the work detail. Moving slowly to allow time to evaluate the pair on the dock, Murph O'Reilly advanced toward them.

"You know how to handle a boat?" He was still half a dozen paces from where Bolan stood.

"Do fish know how to swim?"

The solidly built man grunted a wordless reaction to Bolan's flip response. As Murph drew closer, Bolan noted the network of scars that made the man's face a roadmap of past battles won and lost.

"You handle that tub?" Murph gestured toward the craft where Manny died.

"No sweat." Bolan gave it no more than a passing cut of his icy blue eyes.

"You might just get a chance to do that a little later." O'Reilly made his decision. "For now why don't you shag on up to the day room. That's the big building dead ahead. Ask for Jesse Lobato. Tell him Murph said to put you to work."

Murph turned to leave.

"What about me?" Rick's voice brought the man to a halt.

"What about you?" Murph was one of those who can put a sneer into his voice while keeping his facial expression bland.

"I need work, too. I didn't row this guy all the way out here just so he could get a job."

Murph turned to glare at the upstart kid. Rick's eyes met his and held without faltering. The gang lieutenant gave a little snort and twisted his lips into a half smile.

"I like your style, kid. Shag it up with your partner and tell Jesse I said you're both on the payroll."

"Thanks." Rick's word went unacknowledged as Murph returned to his more pressing problems.

Bolan nodded at Stiles and moved to pass the silent fisherman.

"Got a knife I can borrow?" Stiles's request brought Bolan to a stop.

In that instant Bolan realized the trap the other had set and sprung. Sure he had a knife. In a slit pocket beside his right calf was a stiletto whose twin edges would cut through anything worth cutting. But to produce such a blade, and from such a place, would prove his undoing.

"Use mine." Rick had his own razor-sharp blade out and was extending it toward Stiles.

Without a change in expression the thin man with the chiseled features and hard eyes accepted the knife. For the briefest instant he sawed at a thread on his jacket that didn't need cutting. Then he returned the open knife, hilt first.

"Thanks." As though his words were an afterthought Stiles asked, "How come you aren't working for Warner if you need money? Or even for Tom Devereaux?"

"Bill Welch crews for Tom. And Uncle Ed told me he'd come past the house and pick me up earlier today. He never showed. Maurice came along asking about a ride out here. I decided why not. After all, several of you men are helping them out." He met the eyes of the older man steadily, squarely.

Whether or not the answer satisfied Stiles, he wasn't ready to make a case one way or the other. He turned on his heel and moved to check the pair of un-

enthusiastic men who were sluicing down the blood-
slimed deck of the recently arrived diesel.

Bolan shot the kid a quick glance. Rick responded
with a half wink and flash of his dark eyes. Together
they legged it toward the lighted building twenty-five
or so yards from the line of high tide. Much as both
desired to survey the site, now was not the time.

BECKY DEVEREAUX gave every indication of centering
her attention on the frying pan on the wood-burning
stove. Wilmer Moore, seated at the kitchen table,
knew nothing could be further from the truth. As she
cracked eggs into the smoking pan and stirred them
with quick motions, he knew the little vixen was
thinking of some way, any way, to get free of him.

The clean line of her jaw was marred by a purpling
discoloration. That was from where he had to smack
her hard enough to keep her quiet when he dragged
her into his battered old Dodge half-ton.

Thank the good Lord he had had enough presence
of mind to take off her sneakers while she was still
out cold. Even with the rubber soles she might have
been able to do enough damage to cripple him. As it
was, her bare foot still got to his crotch hard enough
to make him want to clutch at his privates and retch
up what food was in his belly.

The blue mouse under her left eye was her reward
for that kick. He figured they pretty well understood
each other by now. No way would she quit trying to
escape. And no way would he let her attempts go un-
punished. Not that he blamed her. Nor should she

blame him. People did what they had to do. And Wilmer Moore at the age of forty-six was doing exactly what the good Lord must have intended him to do all along.

After half a lifetime of making do with second bests, it was time for Wilmer to better his lot in life. And he was planning on doing just that. It was a caution the way things seemed to work out when a fellow least expected them.

There wasn't a man or woman in Kenlandport who wasn't jumping at his own shadow these days. When Wilmer grabbed Becky, old Tom Devereaux just naturally blamed it on those city crooks out at Eagle Nest Island.

Wilmer allowed himself a brief smile of self-congratulation. Things just couldn't have worked out better. He had known for a long time how to get to all that duty-free stuff down in Boston. He just didn't have the craft to do the job. But Tom did. And once Tom moved his trawler full of suddenly cheap merchandise up the coast to Saint John clear up in Canada, then things would start looking up for Wilmer Moore.

Two, maybe three loads, and he would let Tom off the hook. By then the profits would buy Wilmer a trawler that would put Tom's to shame.

And while old Tom was running his errands, Wilmer would be doing a bit of tidying up at Kenlandport. By the time he blew Bud Stiles and a couple of other fellows to hell and gone, there would be a bunch of first-class lobstering rights and fishing areas up for grabs. Wilmer Moore intended to grab them in both his work-scarred hands.

He detected the subtle shifting of weight as Becky leaned just enough to get set. He let her lay the big fork aside and take the skillet handle in both hands before he broke up her intended play.

"You try to throw that skillet of grease and eggs in my face, Becky, and I'll surely be forced to beat the living hell out of you."

The girl made no reply. She gave no outward reaction to indicate his words reached her ears. However, he saw a gradual change in body stance. Her tensed muscles slowly relaxed and a redistribution of body balance took place.

Yep, the kid had spunk. Lots and to spare. He buttered a slice of whole-wheat bread. His hands did the job automatically while his eyes feasted on the girl's back.

Her black hair was cut shorter than Wilmer preferred. It fell not quite to her shoulders. He would have liked it better had the ebony cascade descended to the middle of her slim back. Wilmer knew the flannel shirt concealed arms muscular from hard physical effort. Her shoulders were broad for a girl so slender.

Wilmer Moore stared at Becky's back as though seeing her trim body anew. What had he read about hostages falling in love with their captors? Why not? Hell, he was still young enough to need and enjoy a woman whose life juices hadn't all dried up. Once he got his ducks in line he might just rid himself of his wife Sarah and get Becky to share his new success. And his bed. Definitely his bed.

Wilmer tensed when she turned to bring his filled plate toward the table. Without so much as looking directly at him she set it before him. Then she turned and brought her own plate and sat opposite him. With her dark eyes fixed on the food, Becky mechanically began to fork it into her mouth.

She wasn't hungry and didn't feel like eating. Yet Becky Devereaux knew she needed to keep her strength up. The next time she tried for the old goat she would be sure to make a success of it. To her surprise the eggs fried in the grease from the ham were no effort to eat. With increasing speed she chewed and swallowed.

What time was it? At least ten and maybe later. She ate last about seven the night before. Becky reached for a slice of bread and a chunk of butter. Briefly her eyes met those of the man opposite her. She held his gaze for just long enough before looking away.

Let him stare. She was used to being stared at. Her flannel shirt did little to conceal the thrust of her firm young breasts just as it did nothing to shorten the slim column of her long neck. They were a part of her just like her chin, which had a tendency to thrust too far when she got her mind set.

Again she reached for the bread and butter. Becky let her dark eyes lock with the murky gray ones of the man who had already bruised her face twice. She kept the contempt she felt from showing in her face. Time enough for that later.

Let him sit and stare at the front of her shirt. He had already squeezed both breasts like a housewife testing peaches for ripeness. But that was while she was tied hand and foot and lying across the worn and cracked seat of his old truck. She had let his disgusting hands touch her. Tied and hurting as she was, there had been no reason to let him know she was conscious.

He wanted to take her to bed right now. She saw it in his eyes, in the slackness of his jaw. Every time he swallowed and worked his throat she knew just what he was thinking.

Becky filled both his cup and her own with steaming coffee without being asked. No need to let him know what she had in mind. Let him believe he had her whipped and broken in spirit.

She returned to sit on the wobbly wooden chair. Though Becky didn't know for sure where she was, she had a pretty fair idea. The Moores owned a worthless little farm about eleven miles inland from Kenlandport. She had passed it many times. Once her grandmother brought her there to pick berries in late summer.

Her thoughts turned again to the man with his reddened face all sticky and prickly from beard stubble. She was uncertain as to whether she would kill Wilmer or let her grandfather do it. Or even Rick.

She wondered what Rick was doing and thinking at this moment. Thinking of Rick caused the line of her jaw to soften, and her chin jutted a trifle less. Rick was an unknown quantity to even those who knew him. But she understood him—which was more than just knowing him.

Though no one, not even her grandparents, knew it, Rick was a hater. He did not hate easily. But once he hated, it was forever. And once he found out about Wilmer, Rick would hate the leering old fool like he had never hated in his life. Even more, probably, than Rick hated the do-gooder judge who let off the drunken driver who had killed his parents.

She'd let Rick be the one to kill the lecherous Wilmer with his three-day stubble of graying beard.

With the future of Wilmer Moore settled in her own mind, Becky drained the remaining coffee from her cup. When she refilled Wilmer's cup she smiled directly into his repulsive face.

Wilmer accepted the smile as his due. Good. She was already coming around.

Minutes later Wilmer pulled his sawed-off twelve-gauge from its hiding place and carefully began to inspect it. First things first. There would be time enough to think about Becky after he settled a few old scores.

9

Jesse Lobato eyed them speculatively. "You say Murph said to put you on?"

"I'm taking over that boat they're just hosing off. It's mine next time it goes out," Bolan said easily. "If it's all the same to you I'll just grab a brew or two and wait until I'm needed."

The offer triggered the response Bolan expected it would.

"Grab a broom instead of a brew, buddy. We go twenty-four hours a day out here. The dirt gets piled up. Get on over and clean out the mess and bunk areas. By the time you get that done I'll have something that will give your muscles a little exercise." He laughed at his own joke.

"What shall I do?" Rick demanded.

"Report in to the cook over at mess. He'll put you to work scrubbing pots and pans or peeling spuds or something."

When Rick hesitated, Lobato raised his chin and his voice. "Move it, kid." Rick moved it.

Bolan knew the broom order for what it was. Let the newcomer understand his place in the scheme of things. That place was at the bottom of nowhere. It was good psychology. He took his time crossing to the sleeping area. His cold blue eyes missed nothing. As hardsites went it wasn't much. But why did it need to be? Open water surrounded it. The Kenlandport residents were believed to be beyond the ability to protest. And who ever stopped to worry about a big guy pushing a broom?

Rick paused before entering the brightly lighted mess hall. His fingers touched the back of Bolan's big hand.

"Keep an eye out for Becky, will you please?" he said as softly as he could.

Bolan signaled his answer with a quick flash of his eyes. The kid nodded his thanks and stepped into the hall.

Bolan took his time finding a broom and dustpan. Once equipped for his cleaning detail, he picked the areas quickly and with care. Open spaces he left to clean themselves. His interest lay in those areas and rooms not readily viewed.

At each closed door he tapped lightly, then entered without waiting for a response. He remained in each only long enough to determine there was nothing of interest inside and to push together a small pile of dust and litter. Once he resorted to dumping a small wastepaper basket to create evidence of work done.

The rooms had a sameness about them, places to sleep with drab, utilitarian furnishings. Few personal effects were present. The troops obviously spent as little time as possible in the cramped cubicles

Midway down the length of the long hall the character of the tiny rooms changed. Though furnished in exactly the same institutional manner, personal items were suddenly lacking.

Okay. It made sense. Bolan figured he was now in that portion of the sleeping quarters used by those on their way into or out of the U.S.

His light rapping was now an automatic ritual. When a muttered response met his next warning knock, Bolan bulled the door open without pausing.

The man who answered the knock was seated at the room's tiny desk. His head swiveled on his thick neck as Bolan entered the room.

"Out! Get out!" The three words, though easily understood, gave evidence that English was not the first language for the agitated man.

Bolan stood his ground and studied the seated man intently.

"Sorry. I was just told to clean out the place." He spread his big hands wide. The gesture indicated he was merely a man doing his assigned job.

Bolan managed to let the broom slip free of his grasp. While retrieving it, he worked at the instant recognition that flashed through his mind when the man turned to face him.

The features were familiar. The wild, staring dark eyes and cleft chin flashed a message in Bolan's memory bank. It was the twisted upper lip that clinched it. The badly healed scar dated back to some poorly-cared-for wound in the man's past.

Marseille. That was the last spotting of the explosives expert who was now coming out of his chair.

His twisted features and clenched hands bespoke the man's agitation at being confronted.

Yeah, the guy was upset all right. But so were the people in that café in Paris. They died when one of his specially concocted bombs filled the normally quiet boulevard with a clutter of bloody body parts and the cries of terrified citizens. Their last sounds made in this life were agonized screams of pain. Yes, and pleas for death to release them from torment they found unbearable.

The guy's name was Claude Monet. Like the great French Impressionist painter. And, in a perverse way, this man was an artist in his own right. Only the images he created were always covered in blood and smelled of death.

Thanking April Rose for the immense rogues' gallery she kept current at Stony Man Farm, Bolan forced his lips into a slack grin.

The grin came too late. Despite Bolan's clumsy dropping of the broom, his wide-spread hands, and the pulled-down knitted cap, the man facing him was no fool. Recognition of Bolan came just as the Executioner's mind found and fitted Claude Monet into his proper niche.

No, Monet didn't recognize Bolan as a specific individual. He could not put a name to the face. Rather he saw in Bolan the enemy, a man whose stand was a full hundred eighty degrees from his own.

Bolan had to give the shorter man credit. He was fast, both mentally and physically. As Bolan straightened up from picking up the fallen broom, Monet spun away from him. He grabbed for an automatic pistol lying on the desk.

Monet's right hand covered the German-made Heckler & Koch Model P9. Bolan sprang to the attack. Stubby fingers were gathering up the pistol as Bolan still lacked two yards of reaching his goal. The bomb maker and dispassionate killer was turning, eager to unleash as many rounds of 9mm parabellum as were needed to stop the big guy.

Knowing he was too slow by a fraction of a beat, Bolan extended his left arm fully. With stiffened fingers, he drove hard into the exposed throat of Claude Monet. The blow's force snapped the murderer's head back. His entire body recoiled in an effort to lessen the force of the attack.

Still coming forward with undiminished speed, Bolan formed his right hand into a lethal plane. He brought it up and across with the entire weight of his body behind it. The inside edge of his stiffened hand caught Monet just below the line of his jaw. It wasn't a killing blow, but it was close.

The H&K fell to the bare floor from fingers no longer able to bear its weight. Bolan came to a skidding halt, preparing himself for his next and final blow.

The eyes of Claude Monet, artist of mutilation and unspeakable horror, met Bolan's and held. No quarter was asked. Hate crossed the short distance between the two men. Yes, and something else. The terrorist's realization that he was not immortal was there as well. Bolan's hand swung in a slashing motion that brought it hard against the other's neck like a huge blade of death.

Monet's eyes dulled at the impact. He collapsed at Bolan's feet.

Confronted with a body in hostile territory, Bolan slid the options past his mind like a deck of cards being shuffled. Removal was desired but impossible. That narrowed his options to hiding the corpse.

Where and how to hide it? Edgar Allan Poe said it best. Hide a thing by putting it out in the open. Bolan hoisted the slack body onto the narrow cot. After quickly searching the corpse and finding nothing of value, Bolan positioned the remains of Claude Monet on his back. With his head pillowed and hands folded across his chest, the man slept the deepest of all sleeps.

There was nothing else in the room the Executioner could put to use. Knowing well the futility and danger of spending valuable time in fruitless activity, Bolan grabbed the fallen broom. He left the room without a backward glance and walked down the hall to the next room.

Suddenly a door opened at the far end of the long corridor. Mack Bolan suspected that time just might have run out.

"Hey, you. Drop that broom and come with me."

Obediently Bolan did just that.

Once clear of the bunk and mess area, Bolan saw that the spot occupied by their dory now held a fishing craft. Half a dozen troops were already unloading boxes and crates. From the look of bent knees and straining arms, Mack was certain the boxes held something heavier than toilet tissue.

"Come on. Hop to it, Cherboneau. Get a move on, man."

Bolan moved quickly to obey Murph's orders. The guy who summoned him from his cleaning task was already part of the work detail. Without being obvious about it, the big guy managed to work his way toward the stern of the craft. Inward relief rewarded the move. Their dory bobbed at the far end of the dock. Tied by a single loose line, it rocked with the movement of the water. From what he could see, its contents were undisturbed.

When his turn came at the head of the line, Bolan accepted a wooden crate with markings in French. Bracing himself to carry the heavy load without loss of balance, he checked the identifying markings. It wasn't all that difficult. In his powerful arms he carried a crate of 5.56mm ammo.

Moving more quickly than the soldier before him, Bolan brought that guy's cargo into eyeball range. He was packing 9mm parabellum loads. Another question answered. These guys were doing more than just moving human cargo in and out of the country. They were preparing for an all-out military thrust.

During the half hour that followed, he served as an uncomplaining beast of burden. He transported arms and ammunition, explosives, electronic devices and a case of premium Scotch whisky that was diverted from the supply depot directly to the day room. Cases bearing markings denoting origins in the Unit-

ed Kingdom, France, Belgium, Italy and Czecho-
slovakia were removed from the boat by the sweating
troops.

The fishing-vessel-turned-gunrunner rose steadily
in the water as the laboring men lightened its load.
Once the final case was hauled over the chipped and
scraped railing, the skipper fired his diesel. Bud Stiles
cast off the pair of lines holding the craft beside the
dock without being asked.

For a brief instant Stiles caught the eye of the
slightly younger man at the helm. Neither spoke. Bolan noted the exchange of glances. The intensity was
not diminished by the plumes of blue gray smoke that
curled from the skipper's stubby pipe. Neither of the
two honest Maine fishermen liked what they were
into. It showed in the meeting of their eyes when
neither thought they were observed.

And something else showed, too. Humiliation at
being forced into doing this job. Resentment at being
brought to heel by a bunch of men whose idea of a
good day's work was shaking down the corner shop-
keeper for a percentage of his profits. Yeah, and
their desire to do something about it.

Mack Bolan did not know Bud Stiles. He did not
even know the name of the skipper who was now so
casually reversing the clumsy-looking craft away
from the dock. But he did know them for the independent men they were. Asking no mercy from the
elements, they survived as men had throughout the
history of the world. For them to be thus reduced in
their own eyes was nearly intolerable.

On the other side of the coin, loyalty to wives and families was big with these quiet, life-hardened men. Just how far they would let themselves be driven out of fear for the safety of their families was a big question. A question Mack Bolan had no way of answering at this point.

Bolan joined the group of grunting cargo movers without becoming a part of them. He stood to one side to study the layout of the site he intended to level before the night was done.

A presence at his side drew his attention.

"Those soft-soled shoes do pretty well on the deck, don't they?" Bud Stiles struck fire to his big-bowled pipe.

"The soles keep me from slipping," Bolan said easily. Every sense was instantly alert. Stiles had shot one bolt and missed earlier. The man was nobody's fool.

Stiles drew on his pipe until an even glow in the bowl rewarded him.

"You keep them pretty clean, considering." Stiles exhaled smoke and let his comment stand.

"Oh, when things get wet and slimy I wear boots."

Again Stiles drew on his pipe. He held the stem tight between strong teeth and held both his hands out before him with their fingers spread. Reflectively he turned them palms inward and pretended to study them. The harsh light of the portable units turned the dock area into day despite the night and fog.

Bolan went along with the charade. Aware that Bud Stiles was studying him, not his hands, he played the game.

He located a cigarette and brought it to life. Stiles eyed the filter tip without comment. The quirking of one of his bushy brows said enough.

"See you barked a knuckle, Maurice."

Bolan studied the big knuckle that still wept blood as the result of contact with a wooden crate.

"One of life's hazards," he said, his voice low.

Stiles drew again on his pipe and appeared to reflect on Bolan's words.

"Life is full of hazards," Stiles said at last.

Bolan let a small cloud of cigarette smoke mingle with the mist. It was Stiles's game. Let him play it.

When the large man at his side elected to remain silent, the Kenlandport fisherman nodded his head as though in answer to an unspoken question. He turned his lean back on the man whose bloody hand he had just studied. Without hurry Bud Stiles walked toward the command post.

Yeah, you can fool some people some of the time. . . . And he had not fooled the savvy Bud Stiles. Not for a minute. First the knife, then the boots, finally the hands. To a man of the sea Bolan's hands were a dead giveaway. Bud's big chapped hands with their cuts and calluses were the battered hands of a man who went to sea in a small boat and hoped like hell he could make a living and remain alive. Bolan's bigger, stronger hands were not those of a working fisherman. It was that simple.

What was not simple was the position taken by Bud Stiles. It is strange what fear does to a man. Especially to a man who previously thought he feared nothing except the gods of the sea and the unknown terrors of an economy based on uncertainty.

Stiles and the skipper whose craft was now lost to view shared a common fear. They also shared other feelings. Which would win out now?

Whether Stiles's fear of the cannibals who infested the island was great enough to cause him to inform on the new man, Bolan had no way of telling. He would like to think the quiet Kenlandport native would keep his knowledge to himself. But there was no way he could be certain.

Sure, Bolan knew he could take the guy out and end the threat. But Bud Stiles was not the enemy. In the end it came down to that. Though he might bring about Bolan's defeat, he still was not the enemy.

10

Rick Cartright crossed between the mess hall and the command post–day room at slow speed. In his hands he held a heaping dinner tray destined for consumption by Big Jim Lane. A clean dish towel covered the tray and its contents.

Midway there, Rick caught sight of Bud Stiles as the lean man approached the door that was Rick's destination. Simultaneously each acknowledged the presence of the other.

Bud veered from his intended path to meet Rick halfway. Rick slowed his pace to a crawl so he could take his eyes from the tray and concentrate on the approaching man.

Stiles did not speak until both came to a halt with less than a yard of clear space between them.

"What are you doing out here, Rick?" Bud spoke around the stem of his pipe with its big charred bowl.

"Right now I'm taking this food to Mr. Lane." Rick deliberately misunderstood the question.

"Not what I mean and you know it. Why are you out here?"

Rick swiveled his head on his thin neck. No one appeared to take notice of their encounter. No one ex-

cept John Phoenix who now lounged against a piling.
Rick could almost feel the force of those icy blue eyes
boring into his very being. The big man missed nothing.

Rick edged forward a fraction, hoping the increased proximity would help to press home the information he was about to reveal to the fisherman. In
quick, terse statements he described what had befallen his uncle as well as what Ed Warner had attempted to do for the people of Kenlandport. When
he ended his brief recitation Rick was aware of a
quiver of lips and a break in his voice. Despite his
best efforts he could not maintain the emotionless
calm for which he reached.

Stiles removed the dead pipe from his lips. Without glancing at it he began to prod the tobacco into
better position. His throat worked. Twice he started
to speak.

At last he jerked his head in the direction of the
dock. Toward Mack Bolan.

"What about that guy?"

"He's with me. He's a friend." Rick hesitated.
"He was the one Uncle Ed tried to contact."

Bud Stiles seemed to give the statement consideration as he again brought his pipe to life.

"You sure he didn't kill Ed?"

"I'm sure." Rick shifted his position. Holding the
filled tray was beginning to tell on the muscles and
tendons of his forearms and shoulders.

For some seconds, which to Rick threatened to become forever, the fisherman sucked on his pipe. But the kid came to a decision. He had to trust the man. Life is based on trust. And if he couldn't trust Bud Stiles, a friend and neighbor, who could he trust? The man dragging on the pipe was even kin. Some sort of distant relation to Uncle Ed. That was the way it was in Kenlandport. Everyone was related to most everyone else by either blood or marriage or both.

"He's okay, Mr. Stiles. I know he is."

"He sure as hell ain't from up north of Rockland." It was a flat statement leaving no room for contradiction.

"I don't know where he's from. Washington, I imagine. D.C., that is."

The older man's chin came up as he gave his entire attention to the youth with the heavy tray.

It was now or never. Trust or fear.

"I know he's not with these guys out here." Rick took in the site with a toss of his head. "He's already killed two of them tonight." Immediately he realized his error. "Make that three. Two on shore and one on the island."

Bud Stiles continued to stare at the boy and suck on his pipe. It did not surprise him all that much. The big fellow had that sort of look about him. He did not panic all that easily. His thoughts came full circle to include the craft circling at full power with three dead men aboard.

"Sure it wasn't six?" he asked.

"Six what?"

"Six men he killed."

Rick considered briefly. "I saw him kill three."

Beyond that the boy was unwilling to commit himself.

"Let me catch the door for you," Stiles said suddenly. His decision was made. "Wouldn't want you to drop the great leader's food on the floor."

Wanting to ask but knowing better, Rick Cartright trailed behind. When the door was held open for him, he entered the room with its haze of cigarette smoke. Stiles did not follow him in.

Mack Bolan started to walk from where he'd been leaning. He sensed the instant Stiles made his decision by an almost imperceptible straightening of the man's body. He only hoped the decision was one favorable to him and to the task before him.

Moving slowly, Bolan reached the point where the dock met the rocky shore at the same time as did Stiles. The two stopped and for a couple of beats communicated only with their eyes. Stiles broke the silence.

"I don't know you. I never saw you before. In fact, I didn't see you on Eagle Nest. Not ever. Just let me get the hell off this chunk of rock before you do whatever it is you came to do."

He halted, seemed to consider, then added softly, "I've got a ship to meet. I'll be bringing in some pretty important men not that long after I leave the dock. At least these people here seem to think they're pretty important."

Bolan waited for the man to continue. Instead Stiles clamped his teeth onto the well-chewed stem of his pipe and deliberately stepped around the big guy.

He had said what he was going to say. He had made his choice. It was all he felt able to do. And all things considered, Bolan could not have asked for more.

For the moment, activity at the site was at a standstill. Those who participated in unloading the cargo were taking what they viewed as a well-deserved break. From overheard scraps of conversation Bolan knew the activity he had observed earlier resulted in a doubling of those on guard. All in all, the site now took on the look of an outpost bedding down for the night. Nothing, Bolan knew, could be further from what was actually happening.

When Bolan moved along the shoreline following his short encounter with Stiles, no one paid any attention to his movement. No one, at least, that he noticed.

The boathouse he had earlier identified was his objective. Walking as if he knew where he was going yet in no obvious hurry to get there, the night warrior shortened the distance between himself and his target. From long experience Bolan knew the importance of timing in any situation involving role camouflage. It could make or break the best or the least likely disguise.

Right now, the trick was to appear as one with the site. Move with the air of one who has a goal in mind, who is executing a task. Show just enough speed to indicate the job is important, but not enough to excite comment or draw attention. It was a fine line and the Executioner knew it.

Though several heads turned and one troop who

passed close to Bolan spoke, no one challenged his right to pass. He eased through the side door of the structure and closed it firmly behind him. He had been careful to look ahead and into the night's misty darkness while moving away from the lighted dock area. His night vision was nearly total when he entered the dark building.

Standing on the board catwalk that ran the length of the near side of the covered landing and storage area, Bolan realized he had hit pay dirt of a sort. The pair of sleek vessels that filled the structure bow to stern were to the lumbering fishing vessels what falcons were to ostriches. The pair of cabin cruisers could be described simply as fast.

Yeah, and ready. Ready and able and willing. Without checking their power plants, Bolan knew beyond a doubt that this pair could deliver thirty knots and more, and could continue to deliver hour after hour. It made good sense. Use the local fishing craft to make deep-sea pickups and deliveries. When a VIP or group of them were ready for transport either south toward Boston or north into Canada, simply fire up one of these beauties and make delivery.

Bringing the recent words of Stiles to mind, Bolan knew he didn't have all that much time in which to act. Slowing the departure of the cruisers would pose no problem. However, it stood to reason that the crew here had mechanics capable of maintaining the costly craft. Therefore a more lasting solution was called for.

Bolan replayed the walk along the edge of the lapping water from dock to boathouse. No way could he expect to repeat it after having visited the dory tied so carelessly at the dock's end. Like a good computer, his brain moved to the supply depot he had just helped stock. And like the capable computer it was, his mind rejected the possibility.

He moved along the wooden catwalk toward the far end, the ocean end, of the long narrow building as he assessed alternate plans of action. There being none better than the obvious, he dismissed the inferior plans and gave his total concentration to what must be done. Yeah, and done quickly.

He stripped off his outer clothing and stacked it out of sight near the end of the walkway. Kneeling, he dipped a hand into the water lapping gently below where he stood. Liquid ice. Bolan slipped silently into the chill of the Atlantic where it intruded beneath the shortened outer doors of the boat shelter.

Bolan swam beneath the big garagelike doors with their overhead openers. Once clear of the entrance, he changed course and headed toward the far end of the lighted dock. The troops showed no hurry in removing the portable high-intensity lights. They were confident in both their location and hold over the local populace.

Using a modified breaststroke, Bolan stayed just below the surface of the frigid water. His black bodysuit kept him all but invisible to those ashore.

Rather than approach the bobbing dory from the sea, Bolan swam directly beneath the far end of the dock. Once under its welcome shelter, he shook the numbing water from his face and hair while treading water with slow, even scissors kicks.

The burbling underwater sounds of Stiles's diesel alerted him to the craft's departure before it began to move. The vessel's propeller churned and whipped the black water to creamy froth. Wavelets and ripples lapped more and more rapidly against the pilings surrounding the man in the water.

Knowing that all attention was directed toward the departing craft, Bolan made his move. After making certain no troops stood directly overhead, he tugged the slack line and slowly drew the broad-beamed dory toward the dock's edge.

Once the boat was at his side, Bolan's long black nylon-clad arm reached over the low railing. Fingers already feeling the effects of immersion in the chilly ocean probed for equipment hidden beneath rotting sacking and canvas. He reached, then reached further. After what seemed at least two eternities of stretching and searching with frozen fingers, the man in the cold sea located what he sought.

A couple of chunks of plastic explosive, secure in waxed paper wrappings, became his. Seconds later the package of detonators and the remote sending device were thrust into one of the numerous slit pockets so much a part of his battle gear. Without looking back he released his hold on the boat. As the dory slowly drifted toward the end of its nylon tether, Mack Bolan repeated his crossing between the dock's end and the boathouse entrance.

Cold, dripping, eager to get on with the task before

him, Bolan surfaced inside the shelter. Immediately he heaved his body onto the wooden walkway. Knowing he left a trail of water on the boards, aware it was a risk unavoidable at the moment, he headed toward the nearer craft. Already he was anticipating his next moves.

The voice from the shadows was as deathly cold as was the snub-nosed .38 Smith & Wesson prodding at Bolan's spine.

"Move and you die."

"Nobody's moving." Again he had underestimated the professional level of the cannibals opposing him.

A lewd chuckle came out of the dark.

"What's that you're carrying?"

"Nitro." The word came easily to Bolan's numb lips.

"In a pig's eye." Disbelief all but dripped from the lips of the man behind the .38.

"Want me to drop it to show you?" Bolan moved both hands forward as though to insure a direct fall.

The guy considered and reached his decision in record time.

"Hold up. Don't do something stupid and get us both wiped. Why should I believe you've got nitro?"

"Why not? What better way to get rid of competition than to lay aboard a charge in each of these?" He gestured toward the two carefully moored craft. Behind him the guy's sharp intake of breath indicated he bought the nitro tale.

"Hey, man, don't wave that stuff around."

"Waving it won't set it off. But the force of a hull hitting the waves will. Or just dropping it."

"What's that you said about competition?"

When Bolan turned to face the guy, the other's only reaction was to step back a pace.

"You fellows don't think you're the only ones looking to make a buck out of import-export, do you?" Bolan let open disdain creep into his tone.

"So where you from?"

"That doesn't matter. It's where we're at that's important."

Yeah, sure. That and the numbers sliding past as though on greased runners.

"Do you go with a winner or do we both die?" Bolan put the decision squarely on the guy with the .38. "There's no way I'm going to swim back out and face the boss and tell him I failed. If I do that I'm dead. And there's no way I'm going to let you take me to your boss. I'm also finished if that happens. So either you let me do my stuff and you come with the winning side, or we both die together."

Indecision ran across the man's ferret-thin face and back again. The weapon's muzzle dipped fractionally.

"Man, my fingers are cold. I don't want to drop this stuff. Here, hang onto it."

Bolan extended his left hand and its contents toward the gunner. Reflexes took over. The guy reached for the "nitro" he could hardly see. Bolan relaxed his grip and the pair of parcels seemed to slide from his opened hand.

The .38 dipped as the guy lunged to save himself. Bolan leaned into the hardguy's forward movement and helped speed it along.

As the harmless chunks of plastic explosive fell clear of grasping hands, a new and terrible danger entered what little remained of the gunner's life. Powerful hands and talonlike fingers caught at head and hair. Massive biceps contracted. Bolan's right knee came up and out, seeking flesh.

The guy's face collided with the unyielding knee in its black nylon cover. His nose and several upper teeth ceased to function as nature intended. Numb from the impact, his mind gibbering about the fallen "nitro," the would-be captor felt his brain turn to jelly from the force of the blow.

Bolan's left hand stayed enlaced in the gunman's thick hair. The fingers and thumb of the Executioner's other hand went on a search-and-destroy mission directed at the exposed larynx of the gasping man. Fragile bones collapsed as a pressure they were never intended to bear closed about them. At his next attempt to inhale, the hardguy was rewarded with lungs full of his own blood. A trio of further attempts and he drowned in his own life fluid.

The plastic, as stable as any explosive, lay on the walkway awaiting Bolan's next move. It was a few seconds' work to scoop up the chunks and stash them aboard the two craft. The stuff was packed firmly into place near the propeller housings of both boats. Detonators were pressed carefully into the puttylike mass, and the job was done.

All that remained was for Bolan to adjust the selective sequencing of the little electronic device and press the red firing-button. But that was for later.

It took precious minutes for him to locate a length of nylon line and a fifteen-pound mushroom anchor near the front end of the building. Half a dozen quick wrappings of the line and the dead troop was ready for his final launching into the dark and uncertain world of never.

As Bolan ran the line's free end through the ring at the top of the anchor, he added the .38 for good measure. Tying the two loose ends of nylon together in a quick square knot, he eased the body over the edge of the walkway. With a minimum of sound, Mack Bolan consigned the body to the sea that filled the boathouse.

Aware that time was speeding by, he hastily slid the worn jacket and trousers over his damp black suit. Not the way he wanted to do it, but the most logical way of keeping the game in play as long as possible.

The trail of dead pointed more and more directly toward the very plank upon which he stood. First Hank lying unattended and unmourned on the rocky shore down from Ed Warner's modest cabin. Then the corpse now stashed beneath the keel-up dory on the town pier.

On the other side of the island a sentry was now getting a taste of guard duty in hell. On a nearby bunk one of Europe's top bomb-makers and maimers of the innocent slept his final sleep. And now, almost at Bolan's feet, rested a hardguy who couldn't think on his feet fast enough to realize that nitro didn't come in waxed paper wrappings.

Bolan cracked open the side door through which he came earlier. Seeing no reason to delay, he again became as one with the fog and dark.

11

The fingers of Wilmer Moore's big-knuckled hand closed about Becky's wrist hard enough to inflict pain. Refusing to show any emotion at his cruelty, yet careful not to antagonize the lecherous man, the girl regarded him with dark, watchful eyes.

"You've made your point. What do you want me to do?"

"Just follow along for the time being." He put his words into action and moved in the direction of the rear door of the farmhouse.

"If we're going outside, I'd like to put my sneakers on first."

His laugh was all-knowing, full of mockery.

"Take me for a proper fool, don't you." The fingers that imprisoned her wrist turned in a twisting motion.

Becky Devereaux flinched at the unexpected increase in pain in spite of her resolve. Imagining no alternative that didn't involve another facial bruise, she followed him from the room.

At first she thought the battered old Dodge was their ultimate destination. It proved to be but a stopping point where Wilmer gathered a red battery-powered flashlight and a pair of wrenches. Seconds later he ordered her to pull open the sliding door of the small barn.

Weathered to the point where not a flake of the original paint remained, the barn leaned as though to avoid a direct confrontation with winter winds. The structure was like those who peopled the desolate area. It was simply too stubborn to give in. It just continued to survive year after testing year.

Once inside, Wilmer thumbed the flashlight to glowing life. The beam circled the dirt floor until it fell upon a length of chain. He tugged the girl forward.

"Sit."

"Here? On the ground?"

"That's what I just said, little lady." He bore down on her wrist to give emphasis to his words.

Becky sat. The earth beneath her was oil-stained and spotted with the drippings and drainings from the crankcases of poorly maintained vehicles.

He shone the light directly in her eyes. Becky's right hand came up to shield her contracting pupils from the glare.

"I'm going to let go of your arm, Becky. I'm going to fit a little iron bracelet around your ankle. It won't hurt unless you make me want to cause it to hurt. But let me warn you, little girl. If you do anything to try my patience, I'll for sure put my boots to you. Do you understand what I'm telling you?"

"I understand." Her voice was low and contained the hatred she'd vowed to hide.

True to his word, Wilmer released her left wrist in

exchange for the corresponding ankle. The suddenness of his gesture caught her off-balance. Unable to get either hand behind her quickly enough to support herself, Becky's head thudded onto the hard-packed earth. He jerked her bare ankle upward to the level of his own waist, keeping her unbalanced and unable to do more than attempt to get her hands behind her.

Cold metal bands encircled her slim ankle. A bolt-hinge joined the two pieces of metal just above her Achilles tendon. They met at the front of the ankle. Wilmer slipped a bolt through the matched holes drilled in the free ends of the metal shackles.

Once the bolt was in place he spun the nut onto the threads until it was finger tight. Then, supporting her heel on his muscular leg, he used the pair of wrenches to tighten the nut. No one with fingers as his only tool would ever loosen it.

Satisfied that he'd done the job properly, Wilmer laid the wrenches a safe distance from the girl. In his right hand he grasped the free end of the light tow chain. In his left he held the flashlight whose beam he directed aloft.

The yellow finger of light caught and held an overhead rafter. Rough cut, the ancient chunk of lumber was a full four by twelve inches. Having supported the upper barn structure for the better part of a century, there wasn't a chance in the world it was not equal to the task Wilmer set for it.

Wilmer bunched the chain's loose end in his big fist. With a casual heave he tossed the fistful of chain over the rafter. It passed up and over the solid piece of wood, then began its descent in a rattle of rust-spotted links.

He let his light locate the chain's free end hanging at chest level. Once Wilmer grasped it in his big hand and tugged, the chain obliged by sliding over the top edge of the rough-cut beam.

Becky felt the shackle tighten on her ankle. Its sharp edges began to cut into the top of her bare foot. To avoid further pain she crab-scooted forward until she was directly beneath the overhead beam. As Wilmer continued to pull downward on the chain, her imprisoned foot and ankle were elevated higher into the air.

When her trim buttocks barely touched the packed earthen floor, Wilmer was satisfied. Three times in rapid succession he fired the loose end of the ever-shortening chain about the beam. Following the third swing he plucked a short length of baling wire from a nail.

Wilmer straightened the eight-inch piece of wire and quickly wove it into the chain's dangling end and one of the links now held taut by the counterweight of the girl's body. He ran the wire in and out a pair of times before twisting the free ends together firmly.

"There." He slid the beam of light the length of the chain that held her leg suspended. "That should keep you out of trouble until I get back."

Becky's dark eyes traveled the chain's length with the movement of the light. Flat on her back as she was, her leg extended to its very limit, Becky Devereaux recognized the futility of her position.

"Don't bother to call for help, little lady. There's

not a soul closer than a mile from here at best. And if I return and find you exercising your lungs, I might just take it into my head to whip your little butt good for disobeying me.''

He swung the flashlight so it shone full in the girl's face. Then he played the light along the length of her nubile young body, licking his lips as he observed her vulnerable position.

''I'll be back directly. But now I've got to slip down to the village to see that your grandpa brought me exactly what he was supposed to. For your sake I hope he did. You're too pretty a child to have to go through life with part of you missing just because old Tom Devereaux was too stupid or too stubborn to follow written instructions.''

He straightened. Then Wilmer suddenly dropped to his knees beside the girl. In her eyes he read something of the frustration she experienced. He recognized the look, having seen it in the mirror while shaving for the last quarter of a century.

Her lips were dry and pressed together. It detracted from the natural beauty of her face. Through a gap in the rough flannel he saw the white lace of her bra.

His free hand slid between two buttons of her shirt and roughly covered the firm mound of inviting woman-flesh. His big, rough thumb peeled back the top edge of her bra and edged onto the creamy skin itself.

In a flash her hands formed claws and raked his face. Though she aimed for his eyes, the man was too quick for her. Instead her short nails dug multiple furrows down his leathery cheeks.

Cursing in a combination of pain and surprise, Wilmer Moore jerked back from her attack. Once clear of her hooked fingers he pulled a soiled bandanna from a pocket and gingerly dabbed at the welts left by her nails. They were beginning to ooze blood into his cheek stubble.

"You'll pay dearly for that, little lady," he said matter-of-factly. A glance at his wrist indicated he lacked the time just then.

Wilmer turned on his heel and covered the distance to the outer door in three long strides.

Over his shoulder he said, "Lie there and think of all the ways a woman can pleasure a man, Becky. Because when I get done down at Kenlandport, you better be ready to pleasure me considerable."

His big hands grasped the heavy sliding door and shot it closed angrily.

Becky Devereaux lay on her back and shoulders in a world suddenly gone darker than she recalled it having any right to be.

Mack Bolan was less than half a dozen paces from the boathouse door when the slim figure of Rick Cartright materialized from nowhere. Keeping it casual, Bolan moved to meet the kid.

"Did you see any sign of Becky?" The kid's voice was harsh and hissing.

"Not yet," Bolan admitted.

"It's no use. She's not anywhere close. I've just

checked the barracks or whatever they call it. Every room is empty except for some guy sleeping in one.''

Yeah. So crazy old Poe was right.

''I've even been over to the generator room. I saw you lugging crates into the supply depot, and you just checked the boathouse. She's not anywhere on the site.

''There's just one other possibility.'' Rick leaned close. ''Clear at the west end of the island, the end nearest shore, is an old cabin. I used to row out when I was a kid and eat lunch there. Once I even spent the night. It's not much, but that's the only place they could have her. I'm going to check it out.''

Bolan stayed the kid with a touch on his forearm.

''Let me do it.'' Doubled guard strength gave the kid little or no chance for rescue even if he did manage to reach his destination.

Sensing Rick's immediate reluctance, Bolan hastened to add, ''I need you here. They've accepted you. Keep your eyes and ears open. We need every scrap of intelligence you can gather.''

He could almost feel the kid's thoughts. The instant Rick reached his decision Bolan sensed it.

''Okay. I'll do it. But get going fast. They're expecting something or someone very important pretty soon. Everyone's already pretty keyed up.''

Rick stepped back half a pace and regarded the big man solemnly in the shadowy light.

''There's a lot of talk about three guys all shot to hell coming in on a boat shortly before we arrived. Did you kill them, too?''

"Do you really want to know?"

"That's why I asked."

"Yes."

Suddenly the kid had nothing to say. Bolan saw his lips part and throat work as he swallowed a couple of times. Finally the kid got some words into his mouth.

"Thanks for going to get Becky. Just be careful. There are quite a few men on guard duty. And watch where you walk until you get into the woods. You're leaving puddles."

With that the kid was gone. An empty tray and white dishtowel swung free in his hands, badges of his acceptance into the group that controlled Eagle Nest Island.

Less than thirty seconds after their parting the Executioner had become just one more shadow in the woods.

Aware that its usefulness was at an end, he shucked the fisherman's garb from his muscular frame. Moving more freely now, the Executioner made short work of the ground between him and the island's shoreward tip. His only regret was that the big, booming .44 AutoMag and the M-3 were still in the dory. Thinking about what you need doesn't put it in your hands, so Bolan gave his entire mind over to what he was doing.

He smelled the pair on outpost duty before he heard them and before the dim outline of the log cabin with its sagging roof showed black against the lesser dark of fog and damp. Overhead the moon tried and failed to peer through the cloud cover and into the fog. For his own peace of mind Bolan hoped the fog would hold and the moon remain only a dim glow. At least for the time being. The night and fog were on his side. And the battle-black warrior needed every ally available to him.

The recollection of having been caught off guard twice previously was still fresh in Bolan's mind. He scouted the immediate area with more than necessary care. Then he closed in on the pair unlucky enough to draw this position on their least lucky of nights.

Satisfied that the two were alone, the Executioner moved forward on silent feet. The pair leaned easily against a wall of the old cabin. The one with the cigar was to Bolan's right. The cigarette smoker stood at the other corner.

When only a scant five yards from the cigar-smoking guard, Bolan pushed his luck no further. From the corner of his eye he saw the faint suggestion of lights on the shore. The fog, as Rick predicted, was lifting.

With the care of a sleek house cat stalking a mouse, Bolan eased the silenced Beretta from its leather home. With movements as careful and dangerous as death itself, he brought the all-knowing eye of the gun to bear.

The 93-R murmured her siren song of death. The guy with the cigar reacted as a 9mm parabellum did unthinkable things to the flesh and fiber that housed his very being. His shattered lower teeth and destroyed jawbone were suddenly no longer capable of supporting the weight of his half-smoked cigar.

As the glowing twist of expensive tobacco fell free

of the destroyed mouth, the second 9mm ripper seemed to follow its course downward. Where the diaphragm separates the abdominal cavity from the thoracic space, a sudden tearing of vital tissue occurred. The slug holed the muscular diaphragm, then angled slightly upward to nick the lower lobe of the left lung. When it exited the body, the jacketed slug punched its path through the meeting point of two vertebrae. The disc separating the two became non-existent as the spiraling slug forced passage through bone, muscle and tissue.

Still firing from a motionless crouch, Bolan sent a similar pair of life-enders toward the unwary guard holding up the far corner of the cabin.

The first offering provided the guy with an additional opening on the near side of his skull. Whether or not the extra ear hole enabled him to hear the delicate strumming of distant harps, or the cries and moans of those in hell, Bolan had no idea. Nor did he care.

Instead of considering the matter, he caressed the Beretta's hair trigger once more. The second time the weapon emitted its whizzing bit of eternity, the deadly parabellum bored its way through a rib and into the guy's life pump.

Savaged red matter was expanding and trying desperately to find an opening, any opening, to relieve the suddenly unbearable pressure. Meanwhile, the guy's heart was having to cope with an inch-long chunk of rib that tore its way through the wall of the right auricle.

Both vital organs reached the same conclusion at the same instant. Life was no longer possible under present conditions. Having come to that understanding, they pulled the plug. The sentry was dead by the time his elbows touched the leaf- and twig-covered ground.

Bolan trod upon both the cigar and cigarette with a twisting motion of his left foot. Then he faced the opening into the cabin that once held a door.

Penlight in hand, he approached the one-room interior with light and Beretta at the ready. Both probed the open space. One with a thin beam of light and hope, the other with an empty black eye that promised nothing better than instant death.

Not wanting to trust the ancient and rotting floorboards, the Executioner surveyed the cabin from the doorframe. There was no need to walk in. Except for some scattered newspapers and an old wooden apple crate, the cabin was empty.

He backed away from the doorway and extinguished the effective little flashlight. So much for that. And so much for any hope of locating Becky Devereaux on the island.

Without pausing to consider the implications of the empty cabin, the man in black blended into the forest. Moving as fast as possible among the trees, he retraced his previous steps.

Even as he planned the next and vital phase of his soft probe now turned hard, a question nagged at the back of his mind. If the girl wasn't on the island, then where the hell was she?

12

Again becoming one shadow among many, Mack Bolan pulled up while shielded from view by the screen of trees separating him from the cleared site. The area housing the small compound had taken on the look of an anthill whose top has unexpectedly been kicked off. Movement of armed guards appeared more for the sake of motion than to accomplish a given purpose.

Yeah, the troops were upset. That much was obvious. Weapons were on open display. Side arms were already in hand. It was as though they expected the Marines to swarm ashore at any minute.

The dock was more crowded than when he left. A weather-worn fishing boat had arrived. Whether or not it was the one captained by Stiles, Bolan didn't know. The increased activity could possibly be intended to impress newly arrived VIPs. It could stem from the discovery of one very dead sentry on the opposite side of the island. It might well be the result of having discovered that a "sleeping" visitor was actually in the arms of lasting slumber. And it could indicate any number of other possibilities. None of them good for the American warrior.

One thing was certain. Standing immobile amid the trees and shadows wasn't going to shed light on the problem. Armed to the teeth as they were, the troops were going to require more firepower than his silenced Beretta could provide.

Having reached that conclusion, Bolan instantly became a moving bit of black among the trees. It took him a few minutes to skirt the site and prepare to enter the water at the far side of the boathouse. Hating to again subject himself to the chill of the sea but knowing no other course of action was open, Bolan slipped into the lapping waves. For the second time in less than an hour the ever faithful Beretta felt the corrosive caress of salt water. As Bolan put the power of his broad shoulders and muscular arms into his under-the-surface stroke, he mentally promised the loyal weapon a thorough cleaning and oiling once the night came to its bloody end.

Taking great care that his hands and feet completed their entire movements below the water's surface so there would be no telltale splashing, Bolan made good time. Whether it was his imagination or his body's reaction to its second immersion in the frigid waters he had no way of telling. Whatever the cause, he found his second crossing more chilling than the first.

A faint glimmer of light on the water ahead foretold another difficulty. The fog was lifting rapidly, and the nearly full moon was trying to light the land and water below. Yeah, it could turn into just the sort of night Bolan didn't need.

He surfaced beneath the shelter of the dock. Without pausing to rest he swam immediately to the structure's end. In what was becoming a standard maneuver, his hand sought the line. Firm pressure caused the heavy dory to begin its second short voyage from the limits of the line to the edge of the dock.

When his free hand located the familiar bulk of the mighty .44 AutoMag, Bolan paused in mid-motion. His mind computed weights, distances and risks in a blur. Then the time factor was entered. The gradual lessening of confusion and noise ashore as men took their positions was the final factor considered. Having weighed all the available information, Bolan made his decision.

Holding his upper body clear of the incoming tide, he slipped the big silver .44 around his neck. The web belt containing the fragmentation grenades came next. Finally the M-3 was hung by its lanyard. The weight of the armaments pulled hard. Automatically he tensed muscles to compensate for the weight.

Before shoving off into whatever battle awaited him, his practiced fingers traced the length of the web belt. The spare clips for the greedy M-3 were still in their canvas pouches. Now all that remained was to put his arsenal to use.

He uncoiled his fingers from the line and the dory immediately began to retreat from the dock. Gripping the underside of the rot-resistant stringers that ran the length of the dock, Bolan inched his way toward shore. After having traveled two-thirds of the length of the dock in this fashion, his fingers and hands were two sets of cramped and frozen talons. But his searching toes finally found the rocky bottom.

While still maintaining hand contact with the overhead timbers for balance, Bolan increased his pace. Within seconds he was at the point where he could no longer stand erect beneath the structure. Ducking his head to enable him to clear the timbers, Bolan emerged from his shelter. Crouched beside the dock, he remained as silent and unmoving as the death he dealt. As far as he could tell, no one was aware of his presence.

Ten yards from where the Executioner huddled in the icy water was a stack of timbers and concrete blocks just past the searching fingers of the incoming high tide. After giving the immediate area a final visual search, Bolan stayed low and covered the distance in a running shuffle.

Once amid the clutter of building materials, he made quick work of getting the .44 AutoMag properly seated on his right hip. The military belt and its precious cargo encircled his waist. He left the M-3 hanging around his neck. Its lanyard allowed the weapon just enough swing so that it could be used immediately.

Yeah, the sight was calmer. It had lost its kicked anthill appearance. The troops had reached their positions and were waiting. And the smoking lamp was not lit, much to Bolan's regret. A soldier with a burning cigarette was easily located by the smell of tobacco. A guard tending his cigarette was not giving one hundred percent attention to the job at hand.

The Executioner noticed that the sleeping area was now fully aglow. At least one end was. The end through which he'd moved on his cleaning detail had its lights on. The newly delivered human cargo was probably there. The absence of sound from the command post–day room gave further indication that the center of operations had shifted to the near end of the living quarters.

Beretta in hand, Bolan left his observation post and took the shortest path toward the shelter of the woods. For a few seconds he thought himself home free. Movement to his right squelched any self-congratulation he might have considered.

"Who's there?" The question was hissed from the dark.

A sentry strained to identify the shadowy figure. Slight though his movement was, it brought him to the attention of stalking death itself.

Twice the Beretta coughed, and the guy manning his solitary outpost ceased wondering who it was that passed in the night. The first slug shredded the trachea just at the hollow of the throat. The second jacketed 9mm death-dealer plowed its course through the right temporal portion of the skull. The guy's brain ceased to function.

Bolan's partial recon of the site brought no more challenge. As he closed in on his destination he ran his eye the length of the long, low building. A light shone a bit past the building's center. Claude

Monet's deep and lasting sleep had become a matter of public record. That, at least in part, explained the increased concern in regard to location security.

Bolan considered and discarded half a dozen approaches. Like so many military tactics, the simplest often proved the most successful. Each additional twist added at least one, and often more, opportunities for discovery or failure.

The man in black moved out of the cover of trees and edged toward the nearest window.

No one challenged him. No alarms sounded. Though he was certain guards were posted within thirty or forty yards on either side of where he stood, Mack Bolan also understood something else as well. Their attention was centered on the woods from which he just emerged. Danger was equated in their minds with the dark and mysterious growth that ringed the site on three sides. The fourth side fronted the sea, a fearful mystery in its own right.

Crouched, moving at quick time, the lean warrior reached the edge of the building. Once certain that no city-bred ambusher was moving up on his position, Mack raised his head to peer through the window. He took in the big room's interior in a sweeping glance.

It was as he suspected. Only worse. Lots worse. Seven new arrivals were clustered together around a small table in the room's southeast corner. They seemed more concerned with bottle and glasses than with the activity in the center of the room.

One guy, obviously in charge, loomed big, dwarfing those about him. Big Jim Lane. April Rose had put a picture of him in Bolan's info folder for him to check on the flight. The hulk now dominating the room was none other than the guy Hal mentioned in his briefing.

Bolan decided at a glance he'd rather not put his considerable strength to a test in physical combat with the monster. Big Jim wasn't fat. He was a mountain of hard muscle. And he was now in a state of anger bordering on frenzy.

The object of his attention sat pale and motionless in a straight-backed wooden chair. Rick Cartright's jaw was set. His eyes were fixed on the face of the giant who loomed threateningly above him.

"Don't give me any of that crap, kid." The poorly installed windowframes proved no barrier to Big Jim's words. "We've been out here three, going on four weeks. Not one sign of trouble. Then you appear and right off the bat I've got a corpse on my hands. And a couple of missing boys. And you expect me to believe you had nothing to do with all this?"

The kid's response was low. His words were lost to Bolan. But his eyes never wavered. Guts. The kid had them by the bucketful.

"Where's the big guy you came in with? Why's he all of a sudden so hard to find?" The hulk's voice was that of one accustomed to being obeyed.

Rick shook his head slowly from side to side. His lips were pressed firmly together in a straight, stubborn line of defiance.

Despite his great size Big Jim had the speed of a

welterweight. His open right hand flashed. Before Rick knew the blow was coming it impacted on his cheekbone. From his vantage point Bolan saw the kid's head snap back on his neck. Yeah, snap back then come forward as the kid reacted. White areas Bolan knew would quickly turn to red blotches appeared on the left side of the kid's face. Rick never took his eyes from the face of his tormentor.

"Where the hell is he, kid?"

Instead of responding, Rick touched his cheek with his fingers. When he did answer, his words didn't carry to Bolan.

A hardguy, the one the others called Bad Louie, extracted a switchblade from his waistband. At the touch of his thumb a wicked five inches of lovingly honed steel sprang into view. He made a quick gesture with the blade in the direction of the kid's crotch. The guy's leer was more menacing than his blade.

Bolan caught Rick's reaction. The kid, if possible, went whiter. Nothing more. But it was enough to indicate his inner fear.

Mack Bolan retreated from the window, inwardly regretting the way things were. If he could only communicate to the kid and let him know it would be okay for him to describe the big guy. To buy precious time for both of them by talking and then talking some more. But there wasn't. The kid was on his own, bound by a code of honor foreign to any other man in that room.

PART OF THE NUMBNESS SHE FELT in her shackled foot
came from the chill night air upon her bare flesh. But
most of it, Becky realized, was because circulation to
her elevated foot had slowed or even stopped.

The bolt-locked bands of metal were not tight
enough to restrict the flow of blood. Her problem
was that the imprisoned leg was suspended so that
her left buttock was actually clear of the ground by a
fraction of an inch. This pulled her weight down on
the bolted device. The twin bands of metal cut into
the top of her foot and heel. This restriction, coupled
with the elevated foot and leg, was slowing the flow
of blood to her tingling foot.

For perhaps the tenth time Becky shifted her position as much as the chain allowed. And again she slid
her hands open and flat beneath her taut, trim buttocks. Resting with her weight atop her spread hands,
she was able to gain a bit of precious height and
relieve some of the pressure on her extended foot.

This time the move proved less successful than the
time before. The homemade shackle refused to slide
even fractionally back along her slim ankle. Desperately she jiggled her foot the small amount allowed
by the all but nonexistent slack in the chain. Nothing
happened. The metal band maintained its position.

Trying to keep her mind from panicking in sudden
fear, Becky Devereaux attempted to recall what she
knew concerning circulation. And the fact that kept
surfacing, over and over, was that prolonged loss of
circulation could result in loss of a limb.

At that thought her body went chill with a cold

that spread from her flat belly upward and outward until it encompassed her mind. The cold seemed to sweep over her, to envelop her total being.

"No!" The sound of her own voice startled the girl. Then, deciding the drafty barn was less lonely for the sound, she continued talking to herself in a calmer, less shrill tone.

"Think, stupid. What would Rick do?"

For that matter, what was he doing at this very minute? Was he thinking of her? Was he worried, searching, frantic?

The pressure of her own weight was once again causing her hand to cramp.

"Lift your butt, stupid. Get your hand out before it cramps up on you."

Slowly, painfully, she shifted her weight to free the protesting hand. As she dragged it from under her rear, her fingers pulled tiny grooves in the packed earth. The short nail on her middle finger was instantly packed with the oil-stained earth.

For seconds she worked with the ball of her thumb in an effort to free the nail of the packed mess of filth and dirt.

When it struck her, Becky quit breathing. There it was. Problems come paired with solutions. But together, they're not always neatly packaged, and you have to find that other half. Rick told her that once, and he was right.

Her numbing foot forgotten in the excitement of discovery, Becky Devereaux began to claw and scrape at the packed earth with both hands.

The shackle responded to her efforts by cutting into the top of her foot. A tiny rivulet of red began to work its way beneath the collar of metal. But Becky felt none of that. With both hands she clawed and ripped at the hard-packed earthen floor beneath her. Even though the dirt had not been turned during her lifetime she began to make inroads into its hard surface. Every bit of dirt she freed, Becky pushed beneath her rump. Within ten minutes she rested on a flattened mound of oily earth two inches high.

When she paused to take a breather, Becky became aware of the biting hurt in her foot. Then the rapid beating of her heart took her attention from the pain. Forcing herself to draw long, slow breaths of air, she gradually stilled the frantic pounding within her heaving chest.

Rodent sounds came again. Becky heard them as she had earlier. The rats, frightened away by her burst of frantic activity, now edged closer. For the moment they caused her no alarm. Much as she detested them, she knew they represented no immediate danger. They would watch and wait. From time to time they might sit up on furry haunches and preen their whiskers in hungry anticipation. But as long as she remained conscious and active they posed no threat. They were a warning of the price of failure.

A digging tool. Her hands explored the area in twin half circles. Nothing. The wrenches were too far away to waste time considering. Not even a broken stick was at hand.

"Don't just lie there like a ninny. Get on with it."

At her own command Becky again began to tear and claw at the time-hardened earth. The watching rodents retreated and eyed the scene with questioning eyes.

How deep must she dig before encountering soft earth? Oh, where was Rick? Why didn't he come for her? For an instant her hands ceased their efforts.

Becky shook her head in a gesture of self-disgust. Her jet hair tossed, then settled in the dirt.

"There's only one place to look for help, girl. And that's right out there at the ends of your arms."

Like twin claws, her hands and fingers formed small but determined scrapers that attacked the earth with renewed vigor.

STELLA DEVEREAUX RAISED her eyes from her clasped hands resting near her teacup to the clock on the kitchen wall. She'd checked it ten times in as many minutes.

"Thomas should have returned by now."

"It's a long run down to Boston and back," Velma Whitmore said.

"He's been gone a long time."

Velma's eyes went cloudy. "Finish your tea. I'll wrap a scarf about my head against the fog and damp, and then we'll walk down to the wharf. We can watch and listen for his trawler."

"Is that a good idea? To be seen waiting, I mean?" asked Stella.

"We can wait and watch without being seen. Tom may need our help when he comes ashore. We're gaining nothing by sitting here and stewing. Let's clean up and we'll get our coats.''

Her sister, grateful for a sense of direction, began clearing the table.

13

Mack Bolan resisted the urge to create an immediate diversion by triggering the remote device he carried with him. Sending one or both of the sleek cabin cruisers into flames inside the boathouse might serve to create enough confusion to enable him to snatch the kid from their clutches. As a long-term tactic it was lacking. No, the kid would have to fend for himself for the time being. That was the way it had to be.

His quick survey of the seven newly arrived men failed to provide Mack with IDs he could pin down. He knew their presence in the country spelled trouble. They were the important cargo the island waited for. Add them to the explosives expert whose career had so recently ended, and the potential for major dirty tricks was great.

His first responsibility was to make certain these cannibals never left the island. Only after that was accomplished could Bolan turn his attention to the twin problems of Rick Cartright and the missing Becky Devereaux.

With his probe turning into a blitz-to-be, the Executioner cast aside any pretense of secrecy. It was hit-and-git time. And God help any who stood in his way.

His wet feet in their damp ripple-soled footgear took the determined warrior toward the building housing the pair of big diesel generators. One of the two roared gutturally as it provided power to light the area. Its mate sat silent and waiting. Separated from the two by the building's wall of cinder blocks stood a five-hundred-gallon tank of diesel fuel.

The fuel tank rested on twin support brackets. They stood atop cement blocks that sat on the ground. Knowing the base was temporary, certain it would be deserted before the coming of winter storms, those who constructed the site left the big tank aboveground. The effort of digging and blasting to place it under the surface seemed wasted in view of the site's short life.

With the exposed tank his immediate goal, Bolan kept to the shadows. He moved rapidly but with an economy of motion, attempting to remain lost to view.

He spotted the guard beside the generator building seconds before the guy was certain the moving shadow was for real.

"Big Jim says to keep your eyes open." Bolan's tone was that of one used to giving orders. And, yeah, having them followed. To the letter or know the reason why.

His hissed order took any initiative from the guy. The guard's spine stiffened as he tried to determine just who in hell was giving him the word.

"And Murph says he wants to know who gave you the idea you could get away with dogging it out here?'' Bolan closed the distance between them and added, ''Just between us, you've got it caught in the wringer.''

Before the other's indignation got the better of him, the Executioner put his fears to rest. The Beretta spat a quick indicator of the guy's real problem across the short distance between muzzle and living flesh.

The guy's lower jaw dropped. It was as though he had mentally framed a reply to the accusations Bolan threw at him but forgot the words.

The parabellum round had no interest in excuses. It twisted its way into flesh and tissue without regard for whether the startled tough guy held up his end of the job or not. The projectile did not distinguish between those who were alert and those who dogged it.

The near-silent body-buster did unthinkable things to the chest cavity and even worse to muscle and tissue as it exited. Its mate left the silenced muzzle in a flash of bright and plowed a trail of destruction through an unprotected cheekbone. The angle of facial bone caused the 9mm slug to veer from its intended course.

Rather than proceed in a straight line through soft tissue and out cranial bone, the slug altered its direction. Combat veterans often report having seen or heard a slug pierce a steel helmet, then encircle the inner portion of the headgear like an enraged hornet seeking a way out. The jacketed missile from the Beretta did exactly that. Only its path was around the inside of the guy's skull.

In making one complete tour of the inside of the skull, the slug created internal havoc only a forensic physician could fully appreciate. Its second tearing circuit ended abruptly when the chunk of life-taking metal encountered the opening of the outer ear. It left the ravaged skull and spent its remaining energies against the block wall close by.

Unaware of the path taken by either 9mm hummer, Bolan stepped around the body of the dead man. With hands made capable by experience, Bolan worked a chunk of plastic explosive free. He fitted it to the fuel tank's outlet pipe. Working entirely by his sense of touch he poked a detonator into place. Then, without needing to check his work, he put distance between the generator building and himself.

A passing worry tugged at Bolan's thoughts. Like a mosquito buzzing around in the top of a tent, it claimed his attention.

Hermann "Gadgets" Schwarz said the remote electronic unit was an all-weather unit. And when Gadgets said something, at least something about electronics, you could go to the bank on it.

"Take this little beauty out in the rain. Use it in a snowstorm. Expose it to dirt and dust. Then, when you're ready to bring hell to earth, activate it. It won't let you down. On that you've got my word."

And his word was as good as gold and better than the dollar. But Gadgets never said anything about dunking it in cold salt water. Not once but twice in the course of an hour. The worry continued to nag. He wouldn't know if he had a problem until he ac-

tually thumbed the device to life. And then it could
be too late. Too late by far if it failed.

Bolan shot a glance at his watch. It lacked two in
the morning by so few seconds they could be dis-
counted. In every battle plan there came a time of no
return. A time when every effort had to be given,
when each pound of thrust must be supplied. That
time had come for The Executioner.

Covering ground fast, this time making no effort
to remain hidden, he retraced the distance to the
lighted end of the living quarters. When the armed
guard on security loomed before him, Bolan did not
so much as pause.

"Hold it, sport! Where do you think you're going?"

In his effort to establish his authority the sentry accepted Bolan as one of his own. Now his eyes widened as the tall man continued toward him without
slowing his pace. Once clear of the shadow cast by
the roof's overhang, the approaching man still remained black.

The skintight battle rig registered at precisely the
same instant the silenced Beretta again uttered its
muted sigh of warning. The warning came too late to
still another who considered himself beyond the law
and who would rule by the power of the gun.

As his optic nerve relayed the muzzle flash to his
brain for analysis, it was already too late for defen-
sive action. A third "eye" magically appeared just
below and to one side of his right nostril.

His free hand, the one not burdened with the military .45 gut-ripper, rose toward the wound as if to confirm its reality.

The second muzzle glow served warning that another parabellum was in flight. It passed through the rising hand and tore two of the heart's four chambers to shreds.

Without needing to check the guy's pulse or listen for heart flutters, Bolan sidestepped the body and ran into the building.

Two beats later he burst into the gathering. Little seemed changed during his short absence. Seven men still surrounded a bottle. Other than that, all eyes were centered on Rick Cartright.

Yeah, Rick had changed a bit and not for the better. The kid's nose flowed scarlet. His upper lip was split. Both his slender hands were pinioned behind the chair's back by a grinning goon.

And Big Jim's face was perhaps a tone or two deeper red. Other than that, it was the same scene.

"We've got troubles!"

Bolan's bellowed words made him the instant center of attention.

"The Coast Guard is right on top of us. They've got a cutter holding steady right off the point. And two landing boats are heading toward the dock at flank speed!"

With every eye now turned toward him, Mack Bolan was well aware it was do-or-die time.

14

Tom Devereaux peered through the thinning fog. Smoke curled in lazy spirals from his pipe with its tooth-marked curved stem. The elderly skipper sucked on the pipe only often enough to keep the coal alive in the blackened bowl.

His faded eyes bleak, Tom turned his head a fraction to study Eagle Nest as it came up on his starboard side. Bastards! The electric power they were wasting keeping the dock area lighted up like a Christmas tree would be enough for the people of Kenlandport for a week. His teeth tightened on the pipe's stem. For long seconds he neglected to draw smoke from it.

Somewhere in that devil's den was his granddaughter. If those animals had harmed her, had despoiled her.... He let the thought and its attending threat lie incomplete.

It had been a day of mentally contemplated revenge. All the way down to Boston, throughout the loading, and during the long haul back up the coast his mind had been only partially on running his craft. Damn and blast them! To take the girl to force him to do their vile bidding!

Who bought and eventually used the cigarettes in his ship's hold bothered Tom not in the least. Whether or not the tax was ever paid on them did not matter. A bit of smuggling never harmed anyone.

But this. Forcing a man to carry illegal cargo in order to protect blood kin. No man deserved to live after inflicting that sort of insult on another.

Tom berated himself for having neither the courage nor the vision to join Ed Warner. After this ordeal ended he would be on Ed's doorstep before the next sunset. Together they would do something to put an end to what was going on. Someone had to act. The pity was he played the part of self-interest too long. Funny how a man's outlook changed once it was his own toes getting stomped on.

Unconsciously his chapped, big-knuckled hand moved to throttle back slightly. Still giving his attention to Eagle Nest's lighted dock, Tom recognized the familiar outline of Bud Stiles's old craft.

Bud was one of the first who started running out to meet the ocean-going ships. Ships, hell. They were rust buckets. Didn't sailors from Panama or Liberia know how to maintain their vessels?

He couldn't blame Bud. How does a man stand up against threats to his wife and kids? He knew they paid Bud something. How much didn't matter. It was all supposed to be some sort of big secret. Well, it wasn't. There weren't any secrets in Kenlandport. There couldn't be. 'Port was like one big, unhappy family in which everyone knew the business of everyone else.

He eased the throttle back another notch. Ahead a few lights shone. Tom Devereaux isolated his kitchen light glinting its welcome through the dissipating fog.

The battered but sturdy dock loomed on his port side. Once more he eased back on the throttle. Docking alone was a bit tricky, especially when the tide was running. But it was not something he hadn't done before and would not do again.

He reversed the propeller. While the brass blades began to churn the water into snowy froth, he hurried to the bow. Almost casually he tossed the looped line over the top of a mossy piling. By the time Tom reached the stern, the craft was just beginning to take the slack out of the bowline.

With practiced skill Tom shoved the craft into neutral and stepped onto the dock. The line found the big, green-stained cleat almost by itself. A couple of quick turnings and Tom wrapped it off in a seaman's knot atop the cleat. After tying off a safety line roughly amidships his work was done.

Tom shut down the idling diesel and stood in the sudden silence. He studied the rocky coast all but invisible in the dark. God, what a hard and cruel place in which to live. But what sort of man would choose to live elsewhere?

Suddenly weary, he tapped his pipe bowl clean and stuck the cold briar in his side pocket. On legs aware of their years he moved the length of the aged dock. Then, with its lights to guide him, he started home.

The old man's steps soon slowed and halted. A thought he had nurtured the entire day without admitting it lived in his mind refused to die. Why did they want him to leave the cargo at the Kenlandport dock? It did not make a hell of a lot of sense. Other craft stopped at Eagle Nest Island. When they came back to home port they were riding high in the water. What if, just for the sake of argument, his cargo was going to be stored somewhere near at hand?

Tom turned, merged with the shadows, and began retracing his steps.

With the moon finally breaking through he would be able to see. He would just find himself a little sit-down spot and see what was going on.

HAD WILMER MOORE been the hand-rubbing type he would have rubbed his big hands raw in self-congratulation. From his vantage point less than fifty yards from the end of the sagging wharf, he saw the *StellaVel* dock. She did not ride all that low in the water, but any fool knew cigarettes weighed less than fish. Besides, Tom did not dare try anything funny. Not the way he doted over his black-haired grandkid.

Working fast, Wilmer backed his old Dodge half-ton right up to the start of the dock. Scarcely daring to breathe, he edged the vehicle slowly, ever so slow-ly, onto the old planks themselves.

With half the distance yet remaining, Wilmer lost his courage and killed the engine. Better not get greedy. Dropping the rear end through a weak plank was not in his plans.

Eager to get on with it, he edged around the side of the truck and all but ran to the waiting vessel. From his pocket he extracted the instructions for Tom's next run. Carefully printed in bold block letters, it showed Tom the time and exact place up in Saint John. He thrust the folded sheet of cheap white paper into the throttle slot. No way it could be missed.

Seconds later he was playing his flashlight over the treasure trove stowed in the hull. As the beam of light located and settled on those cases Wilmer wished to hold on to, he jerked them free of their companions. No need sending everything up to Canada. He had worked it out carefully. Keep some of the best items right here locked safely in his old storage shed. Eventually transport them to the barn out at the farm.

At thoughts of the barn and the treasure it contained Wilmer moved faster. What a night! What a night! Breathing through his mouth, unaware that his heart was racing, he gathered his selected treasures from within the hull.

By the time the truck was fully loaded, Wilmer's thick-chested body was awash in his own sweat. Wilmer eased the old Dodge forward off the dock and onto firm land. Only then did he check his watch.

When would Bud Stiles likely come in and tie up? Stiles would arrive before dawn. He always did. If he tied up sooner, then he could die sooner. If he was late getting in, then Wilmer would just truck the stuff right on out to the farm. And the barn. He never forgot the barn.

Lights off, running in low gear almost at an idle, he eased along the coast a hundred yards or so. After running the half-ton up behind a couple of weathered sheds he cut the ignition.

Wilmer climbed out of the vehicle. Then he turned and dragged the sawed-off twelve from the seat. Taking his time he crossed the open area between his truck and the wharf Stiles always used. After a quick glance about him, Wilmer slowly walked half its length.

Then he sat down to wait. Two loads of double-ought, and Bud Stiles would no longer be interested in his lobster pots. By the time anyone reacted to the shotgun's blast, Wilmer would be long clear.

It was a plan so simple it was totally safe. The thing that made it so was fear. Men who thought they did not know the word's meaning now dropped their eyes when meeting others on the street. There wasn't a chance in the world that those same men would come busting out of their beds to see who was firing down on the wharf. Not a chance.

While Wilmer contemplated his destiny, a pair of slow-moving figures detached themselves from the shadows. They followed the path just taken by the old truck with its valuable cargo.

One of the pair wondered where the man in black, the Phoenix man, was and what he was doing. The other worried that perhaps Thomas might not find the note she left for him. Might not remain at home as the note suggested.

Tom Devereaux was on his feet and moving when the two women appeared from nowhere. Now, like a rubber raft bobbing in their wake, he trailed them.

IN THAT DEAD-SILENT ROOM, Mack Bolan was the center of attention. His words alone were enough to make everyone stop what he was doing. Had they not been sufficient to draw every eye to him, his appearance would have done the trick.

There he stood. Well over six feet of death encased in skintight nylon. Eyes of icy blue that threatened to bore into and through the very sou' of those pierced by their unrelenting gaze. The Executioner's inner presence sent forth emanations that even the least perceptive received and registered for what they were. He was not a man to be ignored.

And had not his physical being caught and held the attention of those within the room, his armaments would. Silenced Beretta in hand, submachine gun hanging from his neck, he was not a figure quickly forgotten. Add to that the massive silver hand cannon riding his right hip and the twin fragmentation grenades dangling from his webbing.

With all those eye-grabbers going for him, it was small wonder none of the troops saw Mack's left hand vanish within the fabric of his nightsuit.

Mack Bolan was not a praying man. At least he was not in the conventional sense. But as his thumb found and stroked the proper button on the remote device, he mentally sent up a word of supplication to whatever gods or fates guided his life.

The plastic explosive erupted the instant he triggered the electronic impulse. The blast ripped the entire side from the fuel storage tank. Bolan's trained ear distinguished between two explosions. To all others it was simply one massive blast that shook the building.

The tremendous heat ignited the secondary blast as superheated diesel erupted in a wall-shaking inferno all its own. The cinder-block wall beside the tank ceased to exist. The roof of the generator room lifted free of its moorings, hung suspended in space, then folded in on top of the massive diesel generators.

Faithful to the end, the monster generator in use continued to provide power despite the wall and much of the roof crashing in on it. When the fuel in its line was expended, however, the gallant machine ground to a reluctant halt.

Those confronted by Bolan remained suspended in time as the two-in-one explosion rocked the building and assaulted their senses.

"The Coast Guard is firing on the site!" His words were deliberately loud to penetrate dulled senses. "They've opened fire on us!"

At that instant the room's lights dimmed, then everyone was engulfed in total darkness.

"They've hit the generator! The place is on fire!"

The room erupted in an explosion of its own. Voices were raised in question and in protest. Big Jim Lane bellowed to make himself heard above the tumult.

"Louie! Hang onto that kid! Don't let him get free! The rest of you—stand fast! The emergency lights will be on in a second. Stand fast, I said!"

His final words were in response to a body that plowed its way from the drinking table toward the dimly outlined window. Despite Big Jim's orders, the man, a taker of hostages and raper of women, launched his body through the glass and into the night.

As though in reaction to Big Jim's words, the battery-powered emergency system brought light to the chaotic room. A pair of lights mounted above the room's two entrances provided sufficient light to enable Big Jim to rally his troops.

His first glance was toward the entrance leading outside. The big devil was gone. No problem. They'd get to him later. And when they did. . . .

His second look was directed toward where the kid was last sitting. He was no longer sitting. Now he was standing up, the kid's entire weight on his toes as he tried to rise even higher to escape the punishing pressure as Bad Louie twisted his tortured arm ever more tightly. Good man, Louie. He was one of those guys Big Jim knew he could depend on.

"Hang onto him." His blazing eyes served to punctuate his words.

Louie nodded his understanding.

"Jesse."

Lobato's head came up.

"Take about half these soldiers and see about getting that fire under control." Through the room's seaward windows they could all see smoke and flames boiling into the night sky.

"You got it." With a combination of head jerks and a stabbing of index finger Lobato indicated those who were to accompany him.

As that portion of the group made a quick exit, Big Jim gave his attention to the men still grouped around the drinking table, then his eyes did a quick tour of the remaining troops.

"Fish, pick three or four guns and make certain the rest of this building is secure. Post them down the hall." He jerked his huge head toward the far end of the building.

"Once you've secured the area, get your butt back here. These guys—" he gestured with his shaggy brows toward the table "—are your responsibility. Nothing, and I mean nothing better happen to them."

Fish indicated his understanding by a flash of white teeth marred only by the absence of one canine lost in a misunderstanding concerning a payoff. The misunderstanding was settled, but not before a store owner extracted the canine with the business end of a claw hammer. A couple of Fish's boys returned the favor, and now the owner gummed his food.

Using his chin as a pointer, the loyal soldier selected a quartet of guys he knew could handle themselves. Without glancing back the detail moved out.

Big Jim mentally checked off those things that needed doing. Only one remained. Get that big bastard.

"Boss." Bad Louie's tone was tentative.

Big Jim fixed him with a glare.

"What about the Coast Guard?"

"Hell!" How could one of his troops be so stupid? "There ain't any Coast Guard out there. That dude in the skintights set a bomb. Don't be such an ass.''

To cover his chagrin Bad Louie tightened the pressure on the kid's imprisoned wrist. The kid came to the very tips of his toes. A moan ripped from between his split lips. Bad Louie felt better.

15

Bud Stiles had a ringside seat for the action. Other than the soldier who confronted Bolan at the entrance to the living area, Stiles was the only man who saw Bolan begin his blitz.

When Stiles saw the guard slump in reaction to the pair of quick muzzle flashes, he realized that an unpredictable chain of events was beginning. Without undue haste, yet with no wasted motions, he slipped the bow line free. The front of his vessel began to move slightly clear of the dock's edge.

Next, he pulled a razor-sharp hand ax from its safety clips and placed it within easy reach. Seconds later he thumbed the starter. The dependable diesel came to life without protest.

Secure in the knowledge he had done all that was necessary, the soft-spoken skipper turned his attention to the door through which the big fellow had run.

When the fuel tank blew it was like those pictures of hell Stiles recalled from his Sunday-school days. In awe he followed the orange fireball skyward. For more seconds than he thought to count, the ball of flame hovered above what remained of the generator building.

Then in an impossible display it began to rain liquid fire. If that was the way it would end, it was sure going to be one hell of a show when Judgment Day rolled around.

Despite the fear that originally coerced Stiles into lending his boat and skills—plus the money he was getting—he was a practical man. And common sense dictated his immediate departure. That group of worthless scum he had just delivered, and the one hard-eyed creep he brought in earlier, would have to find other transport to the mainland.

His fingers curled about the throttle. The lever slid the entire distance to the stop. In response the propeller began to thrash and churn.

Bud Stiles grabbed the ax at mid-handle. He brought it up and then down in one fluid motion. The blade severed the big line and buried itself in the rail.

He figured it would be better to replace the line later than to waste precious time freeing it from its cleat at that moment.

Only when a hundred yards of open water separated his craft from the dock did Bud Stiles look again toward the island. It was a shame about those big generators. By the time that hellfire burned itself out they would not even make good scrap. Dourly he observed the figures highlighted by the dancing flames. Not a chance in hell they would be able to douse the fires. Contain them, maybe. Probably save most of the other buildings. But the diesel-fed inferno would continue to brighten the night until it felt like quitting.

He filled his lungs with sea air. Slowly, thoughtfully, he let the good, clean air escape, puffing his cheeks as it passed.

Those poor bastards on Eagle Nest didn't know it yet, but they had just about spent their last nickel. He didn't know who that big guy with the soul-probing eyes was. Did not want to know. Not now, not ever. But one thing Bud Stiles did know. If he was doing something and that guy told him to stop doing it, Bud would stop. Stop and never, by God, start again.

He considered the situation and cut back on the throttle until the wide-beamed craft was barely holding its own against the crosscurrents. He dropped a lashing about the wheel and crossed to reach beneath the chart table in the tiny wheelhouse.

When he straightened, Stiles held an AK-47 in both hands. He did not need to check the assault rifle. It was primed and ready. With the stolen weapon tucked beneath his right arm he returned to the helm.

He put fire to his cold pipe and gave his attention to the island, eager to see what other surprises the big guy had planned for that bunch of bloodsuckers.

AS ONE WITH THE FRIENDLY DARK, Mack Bolan slammed the Beretta into her leather. Without wasted motion he gathered the waiting M-3 into his hands. Leaving the stock for another time he prepared to use the stutter gun almost like a machine pistol fired two-handed.

By the time the emergency lights brought an internal glow to the mess hall, Bolan was ready for the second phase in his planned blitz.

When half a dozen troops streamed from the hall toward the hovering diesel fireball, the Executioner was awaiting them. With the M-3 spewing between six and seven rounds of 9mm challengers every second, he gave them a quick crisscross move of the barrel.

When two of the six still showed signs of fight, he did a quick figure eight on both of them. For effect he let the final rounds flow through the barrel in the general direction of those hurrying toward the remains of the power plant.

Bolan slammed home a full magazine while running toward the rear of the mess area. There, gleaming like dull silver in the reflected glow of the blaze, was Bolan's goal. The propane tank silently awaited its opportunity to make a contribution to the conflagration.

Behind him startled troops called out to one another. The sudden chatter of his M-3 from out of the night was doubly terrifying due to the lack of muzzle flash. With the flash hider doing its job, Mack Bolan was all but impossible to spot even as he hosed death from his weapon.

The Executioner faced the waiting propane tank. He would rather have done the job from well back in the woods. But time was going by too rapidly to take even the few seconds necessary to put trees between him and the waiting bomb.

And waiting bomb it was. As he slipped the mighty .44 AutoMag from its holster, Mack Bolan knew full well the danger he courted. He knew yet willingly accepted the risk.

At a distance of no more than twenty-five yards he

brought Big Thunder to bear. A stroking of the weapon's trigger, and hell on earth was unleashed for a second time in as many minutes.

The 240-grain body-buster became 240 grains of detonator. As the massive slug impacted with the pressure-strong metal of the propane tank, Bolan threw himself flat on the ground. The entrance wound created an instantaneous spiderwork of cracks in the thick hide of the tank.

Half-filled with explosive propane, the volatile mass of pressurized gas awaited any excuse to escape its manmade prison.

Sparks flashed from the .44's entry. Too fast for the eye to discern, some 250 gallons of cookstove fuel expanded to a hundred times and more their original volume.

The tank's plating became thousands of high-velocity bits of shrapnel. Some spent themselves harmlessly in the earth. But a major portion of the tank's casing scattered to all points of the compass in a lethal hail of instant death. Bolan, belly pressed to the earth, felt jagged chunks of metal whizzing above his head. A guard on security patrol near the command past was not so lucky.

At the same time the blinding flash of exploding propane was imprinting itself on the guy's retina, a piece of heavy tank casing was on a collision course with his right thigh. It did not just embed itself in his hulk. The rampaging shard of terror tore through the upper thigh. Jagged edges ripped out flesh and muscle with the speed and power of a shark attack.

Stunned by the mule-kick force of the blow, the guy stared at his savaged thigh without comprehension. So great was the physical trauma of the blow, the soldier remained unaware that a second, smaller chunk of instant death had made itself at home in his throat.

Blood was spurting in uncontrollable quantities down his chest before the guy realized what had happened. By then the scooped-out area of his thigh was welling crimson as well. Whimpering, attempting to cover the gaping wound with both hands, he sank earthward.

Four other of the site's defenders absorbed screaming chunks of the deadly shards in various parts of their bodies. None received wounds that were immediately life-threatening, but neither did any of the four find their physical condition improved by the chunks of propane tank embedded within living tissue.

The propane ball of fire put to shame the previous efforts of the diesel fuel. Glowing yellow scarlet, it climbed from its launching pad to brighten the sky only just beginning to dull from the earlier explosion.

Once certain he was still in one piece, Bolan came to his feet on the run. Big Thunder again found itself in the flapped holster. Again the M-3 with its obliging flash hider was grasped in a pair of determined hands.

Combat fighting, like everything, operates according to certain rules. The advantage goes to the force able and willing to surprise the foe. And once an advantage is achieved it must be maintained. So it was with Bolan's blitz.

He had scouted the area sufficiently to know where and how to strike best. He had achieved total surprise as he burst like a messenger of death and destruction into the very midst of the enemy camp.

Now to maintain the advantage so quickly gained. While confusion still reigned, before the scattered and shattered troops could rally, he intended to hit them again. Again and hard. And where it counted.

Bounding from the light shed by the flaming propane, Bolan double timed it toward the command post. Someone spotted his distinctive form in the noon-bright glow of the hovering fireball. The heavy reports of a .45 called attention to the quickly moving figure. The lighter cracks of more than one .38 took up the cry. Not to be outdone, the easily recognized chatter of an AK-47 added to the clamor.

Bolan dropped to a knee and replied. The M-3 added to the chorus of death until it had run through its entire thirty-round clip.

He again moved out in a crouching run. By the time he had advanced eight or ten paces, the glowing ball of heat was losing some of its brightness. Three troops were also missing much of their former sparkle. All found it difficult to direct their weapons with 9mm parabellum missile punctures in their bodies.

One of the three found it impossible to function after a single round ripped through his aorta. A second clutched his shattered kneecap and screamed in agony. He had no recollection of his delight a year before when he held a victim while Bad Louie used a baseball bat on that unfortunate's kneecap.

The third victim of the Executioner's indiscriminate spraying by the M-3 couldn't, at first, believe his luck in having avoided contact with any of the thirty rounds. Other than a numb left wrist he experienced no injury.

It was only when his numb wrist began to leak onto his shoe that he realized his good luck was a joke. His left hand remained attached to his body by a half-inch-wide band of bloody flesh. In horror and disbelief the guy lifted his arm for a better look. The hand slipped to hang at a right angle to the arm and wrist. The wrist pumped and poured scarlet from severed artery and vein.

The hardguy who was able to grin while putting the boots to a car owner behind on his payments, fell to the ground, his head resting in a pool of blood.

Two sentries, drawn by the sound of battle and the fury of the flames, came in from the site's perimeter and met the Executioner almost head-on.

"VC!" The first to see Bolan, who was still moving with a fresh chamber of horrors in his M-3, uttered a cry from out of his past.

As the sentinel swung his Thompson toward Bolan he again cried his warning:

"VC! Dead on!"

The living shadow eased back on the trigger and did a quick figure eight, literally stopping the guy dead in his tracks.

Bolan then turned his attention to the less observant of the two. He poured half a dozen rounds of jacketed death into his chest at point-blank range.

Any eagerness for battle the man possessed was lost in the second he was a target.

Dead while still standing, his thoracic cavity only a memory, he did a quick stumbling retreat. Without having fired a shot, he joined his fallen buddy.

Bolan swung on his heel and headed toward his original target. Just ahead the command post–day room waited. Its interior glowed with the light of a pair of battery-powered emergency lights. The radio operator sat in confused indecision. Should he join in the pitched battle erupting outside? Or should he remain at his post in the event Big Jim needed him?

It was Death, not Big Jim who sent for the undecided operator. A grenade flew in the opened screen door. Pin out, spoon free, it rolled and scooted from the door directly toward the radio and its operator.

In one brilliant flash the rig became an unrecognizable tangle of wire and metal. And in that bright-white instant the guy's indecision ended as well. Both his life and his lower limbs left him in one searing explosion.

Overhead, one of the emergency lights absorbed a chunk of the grenade's casing. Its light failed. Across the room its mate continued to cast a glow into the room suddenly gone foul with the sight and smell of death.

Knowing he had made major strides in neutralizing the effectiveness of the site, Bolan turned again toward the living quarters. Stunned, intent upon their own survival, none of the troops still fit for combat challenged his passage. It was as though the smoke and flame and human wreckage made the black-garbed man invisible. Some simply wished not to see him. And by wishing could not.

Bolan came through the open door with both hands filled. In his right he bore the big .44 AutoMag. In his left was his second fragmentation grenade. Pin gone, its spoon held down only by the pressure of Bolan's grasp, the grenade was potential death awaiting an opportunity.

While chaos reigned through most of the island hardsite, those within the large room appeared calm, almost divorced from the death and destruction only a wall away.

Rick, his face pale as blood still seeped from his nose and caked on his lips, managed a welcome flashing of his eyes.

"I've come for the kid."

Bolan let them all take a good look at the grenade and at the big silver AutoMag's gaping eye of death.

"You want him in chunks or slices?" As Bad Louie Stevens spoke his final words he waved his switchblade just beneath the kid's ear.

Bad Louie did not realize that death picked his name. That was a pity. Bad Louie always gloried in letting others know that their deaths were near at hand.

The 240-grain heart-stopper did its job. As an added bonus it all but exploded Bad Louie's faithful pumping organ. Bits and pieces of cardiac muscle mingled with lung tissue. Bad Louie released his hold on the kid's uptwisted arm and fell to the floor.

Rick sank from his tiptoes to his heels as his tormentor collapsed. Bad Louie made one final attempt to draw air into shattered lungs and failed. The hardguy who thought a switchblade made him a man stopped breathing. Blood trickled from Bad Louie's one good nostril along with his last breath.

Without having to be told, Rick moved toward Bolan and the door. His calf muscles, pressed beyond reasonable demands by his forced on-the-toes stance, threatened to fail him. He bent double and massaged one, then the other, with both hands.

"Can you make it?"

"I'll make it. One way or another I'll make it."

Bolan's steely blue eyes surveyed the group. No one seemed inclined to argue. Even Big Jim Lane was at a loss for words. The memory of the silver handgun's booming thunder was too fresh for any to dispute the man in battle dress.

"The kid and I are walking out of here. Anyone who thinks otherwise, now's the time to speak."

No one spoke.

The two of them slowly backed from the room. Mack Bolan with both hands full of death covered the retreat of the skinny kid who possessed the nerve of one to whom the notion defeat was completely foreign.

16

Jesse Lobato recognized the man outlined by the light that spilled from the open door of the living quarters. Leaving the few troops with him to their futile task of controlling the diesel fire, Lobato unleathered his revolver.

He covered ten yards in a running crouch. The bastard in black was moving slowly. At his side a slim shadow limped and staggered. The two targets were moving in almost a direct line toward the dock.

His lips pulled back in a mirthless grin. They came in a dory but they would leave in coffins. He began to edge forward, wanting to close the distance between them before opening up with his .38.

A sentry, fresh from duty in the woods, burst from cover. His AK-47 began a from-the-hip scattering of 7.62mm gut-rippers in the general direction of the retreating pair.

Silently cursing the fool, Lobato brought his own weapon to bear. Directly ahead of him, the guy in the tight nightsuit spun to face the chattering assault rifle. Lobato saw him bring that huge hand cannon up and around.

As Jesse's ears objected to the rolling thunder of

the big weapon, he caught sight of the oncoming sentry from the corner of his right eye. The soldier was no longer moving forward. It was as though an unseen hand reached from nowhere and slammed the guy back on his heels.

The huge handgun boomed its anger again. And once more Jesse saw the effects of its heavy, gut-wrenching slug. The AK-47 flew from the sentry's hands as though snatched by supernatural forces. The round lifted him onto his toes before flinging him backward in a clumsy back flip. Lobato knew the guy was dead while still in the air.

A range master might have forgiven Jesse when he tugged the trigger sharply. His first shot jerked wide to the right. Before he could get the blade of his front sight square with the notch in the rear, it was too late. The Executioner was not forgiving.

Bolan saw his first 240-grain skull-buster do what it was supposed to do. Like a ripe melon, Lobato's skull erupted in a spray of gray matter and gore. Bits and pieces of skull and scalp rained to earth. From his upper jaw to the top of his slightly balding head, Jesse Lobato ceased to exist. The .38 dropped from hands that no longer cared to hold the weapon.

Rick stumbled on a few paces before coming to a halt. With eyes gone numb he viewed the carnage.

"Come on." Bolan's voice, while gentle, held the firmness of command.

"My God." His voice held awe and disbelief. "You did all this."

"War is never pretty. Now let's get a move on."

The kid remained unmoving. As one is often terrified by a horror movie yet unable to look away, he kept sweeping the area with his gaze.

Figures filled the doorway and burst into the night from the building they had just left. Big Jim Lane directed a guy with a thrust of his hand. The man let fly with a Thompson .45.

Bolan snapped off a quick round with the Auto-Mag. The gunner forgot about continuing his .45 fire as his belly exploded in ripping pain. Clutching his middle he sank to his knees while Big Jim sprawled on the ground, clawing for safety.

Rick turned and headed for the dock. The kid was moving better. The strained calf muscles were loosening a bit.

Twice more Bolan had to turn and let Big Thunder's roaring voice warn off pursuit. Backing away from one such effort, Bolan collided with the kid. Bolan spun the kid and roughly propelled him toward the dock.

"Becky! What about her? We can't leave without her!"

"She's not on the island. She probably never was."

"Then where is she?"

"On the mainland."

"But why?" the kid demanded.

"We'll find out why and where when we reach shore," Bolan said.

While the kid pulled the dory close enough to board, Bolan let loose a pair of blasts to discourage anyone stupid enough to want to venture closer. The grenade described an arc in the night and rained death on a hardguy more foolish than brave.

The kid tumbled aboard and started slamming oars into their locks. Bolan followed. The line parted when the big .44 roared 240 grains of line-cutter into it.

While Rick bent to his task, Bolan slapped a fresh clip into the AutoMag. He brought the M-3 to the limits of its lanyard without a wasted motion. Elevating the muzzle high enough to clear the dock above them, Bolan's trigger finger tightened.

The M-3 chattered until its entire thirty-round vocabulary was exhausted. Bolan's ice-blue eyes detected movement as troops regrouped. But no one was eager to charge to the end of the dock.

BUD STILES THANKED THE FOG for lifting to allow him a good view of the destruction of the cancer on Eagle Nest Island. Overhead the moon shed its cold light on the site made hot to the point it gave its defenders a foretaste of hell.

As Rick Cartright moved the heavy dory through the light chop of the water, Bud extended his mental congratulations to the lad. The boy was all man.

He'd never seen anyone like this big fellow. At least Bud had the presence of mind to get the hell out of there before that one-man army let loose. And what a job he did! Not that it was over and he was home free. Not by a long shot. From Bud's private box seat he saw frantic activity.

Nope, Rick and his newfound friend still had a hell of a problem. And unless Bud's eyesight had suddenly gone bad he saw problems—make that two problems—forming up right now. The boathouse was alive as those slimes Bud just delivered were hustled aboard that pair of racy cabin cruisers. But that wasn't what really mattered to the guys in the dory.

Not really. What really spelled the end of the world was Big Jim Lane's private craft. The one just now having its tarps slipped free way off to the port side of the dock. With its twin inboards, that twenty-six-footer could run the paint off of any craft for twenty miles in either direction up or down the coast.

Put six or eight hardnoses with automatic weapons aboard, and that thing could have tackled the Spanish Armada.

Aware that he was as visible to those ashore as they were to him, Bud Stiles slipped the throttle forward a pair of notches. The aging diesel responded.

A minute later Bud slid the throttle forward one more stop. No sense getting caught in the crossfire. And it sure made no sense having those cabin jobs come alongside and order him to take that cargo of human sewage aboard.

He gripped the AK-47 for what assurance it offered. Well to his starboard and slipping rapidly astern was the heavy dory. For just a passing instant Stiles considered bringing the bow around and picking Rick and the monster man out of the water. Then reason prevailed.

He advanced the throttle one more notch. There

was no saving the war machine and the boy at the oars. And dying himself for what was already a lost cause made no sense at all.

THE TEARS IN HER DARK EYES were those of total frustration. With chest heaving from her efforts Becky let her bottom settle on the mound of dirt she had clawed from the barn's stubborn floor.

Her nails were split and broken. The tips of her fingers were raw and weeping blood. Her foot was raw from its constant contact with the biting edge of the shackle. It, too, seeped blood.

There had to be some way out of this. All she needed was to be able to reach high enough to get her hands on the twisted wire. Untwist it, swing the chain's loose end over the beam, and she would be free. At least free to the point where she could fumble around and locate the pair of wrenches.

She felt the earthen mound. At most it was not more than a foot high. Lying as she was with her rear end up higher than her head, she was very uncomfortable. Worse, if Wilmer returned and found what she had been up to, there was no telling what torment he might dream up for her.

"Okay, kid, it's now or never." Her words took on a hollow sound in the empty building.

A trio of watching rats scurried a few feet at the sound.

Becky brought the upper portion of her limber body erect by placing her arms straight back and extending them. She drew air into her lungs, held it, then puffed it out. Twice she repeated the process.

Holding her body upright with her right arm, Becky fumbled for the chain with her left. Her efforts again pulled the edge of the shackle into the raw cuts atop her foot. Gasping from the pain, Becky caught the chain above her imprisoned ankle in her left hand.

Becky counted steadily from one to five. On the count of five she pulled her right hand free of the earth. Lunging with all her strength, she caught the chain with her right hand. Pulling upward with both hands on the chain, awkward due to her raised leg, the girl got her free foot under her. It sought and found the earthen mound. She gave a little cry of triumph.

Once Becky got her balance she stood on one foot, clutching the chain in both hands. Quickly she raised her hands along the chain to the limits of her reach. Too low. She still could not reach the length of baling wire interlaced with the chain's free end.

"Now what?" She knew the next step, the only step. It was just that by asking the question aloud, Becky gained time before having to face the inevitable.

Again she went through the deep-breathing routine. She bent her supporting leg to the limits allowed by her chained ankle. Dreading the pain she knew must follow, Becky lunged upward. Her hands clawed at the chain links, slipped downward, then tightened. The force of her upward spring all but tore the chain from her cramped and tender hands.

Clinging to the chain, clawing her way upward, Becky found herself mouthing half-formed prayers. She did not know whether she was progressing or whether her struggles were doomed.

And then her trapped ankle was under her. The metal shackle slid upward on her ankle as her weight pressed down into it. With both hands tight on the chain she hauled her body upward. Suddenly she was able to straighten her leg. The shackle rose on her ankle until it caught on the swell of her calf. And there it held.

Becky's weight drove the metal's edge into the front of her shin. She stifled a scream and only whimpered as the intensity of the pain brought tears to her eyes. For a few seconds Becky held tight to the chain as she supported part of her body's weight with her torn and bleeding hands.

The shackle's edge bit into her flesh and opened a new wound. For a moment Becky all but laughed aloud at the insanity of the situation. And to think how she had hated a thin line of scar on her shin. The one she put there with a razor two years ago while shaving her shapely legs. Well, the scar she was making now would be one she would remember the rest of her life.

Slowly the chain began to turn. The motion did not bother her. The only important thing now was to locate the twist of wire. When her probing fingers found the wire's sharp-pointed end, Becky flinched at the sudden pain. It was like a needle being thrust into her already bleeding finger.

With the cuff of iron biting into her shin and calf, Becky traced the wire's path. At least Wilmer had not used a pair of pliers to tighten and bend back the ends. Mindless now of the pain, Becky Devereaux began to untwist the wire's twin ends.

One thing was certain. She did not dare let her leg betray her. No matter how much it hurt, no matter how the chain spun with her clinging to it, she must not let go. The girl's mind told her there was no chance in the world she could ever again clamber up the chain.

Damn that Wilmer Moore! Damn him to hell everlasting! As she fought the twisted wire Becky relented in her desire to have Rick kill the man. No way. She would do it herself!

17

The way the dory bit into the water's rough chop, Bolan knew the kid was putting everything he had into the oars. Everything and a bit more.

Bolan slapped another full magazine into the M-3 after pulling the lanyard from around his neck. He eased the freshened chatter gun onto a chunk of old fishing net at his feet. It was the big .44 AutoMag in which Bolan was placing his trust and their lives.

Lights gleamed as the boathouse doors opened into the night. Bolan permitted himself what might have passed for a quick smile detected only by the inner man. The men were forced to jimmy the doors to free the sleek cruisers. When the power went so did the electric motors that operated the door openers.

It was just one more instance in which modern man trusted too much to uncertain technology. There was a lesson there for the learning. Bolan doubted that the men who strained to force the doors were in any mood to learn.

Almost as one the two cabin cruisers roared into the night. Though he was in no position to see whom the craft carried, Mack Bolan knew something of the importance of their cargoes.

Specialists in terror, bomb-planters, those who traded in fear and human suffering. Yes, precious cargoes indeed. And why were they suddenly being channeled into an unsuspecting nation? What made their free and unopposed passage into and out of the United States so important that a village of citizens had to feel the bootheel of terror hard upon their throats? It was a question the Executioner could not answer.

Rather than waste valuable mental energy seeking an answer without sufficient input, he pushed the whys and wherefores from his mind. Instead he found the setting on the remote device, which was indeed an all-weather implement. Gadgets Schwarz would be happy to learn that immersion in salt water did not affect its capabilities. Happy, hell. The electronics genius already knew.

Bolan thumbed the control. By feel he readjusted and thumbed again. The first cruiser's brilliant demise lighted the way for the second. Quick on the heels of the first blast came its companion. The carefully positioned plastic explosive charges did their job and more.

By the light of the first flaming craft Bolan saw the second's stern lift free of the water. Dark shadows, which could only be bodies, assumed impossible positions as they were airborne. Flailing arms and legs testified to the force of the explosions.

Behind Bolan the kid missed a beat with the long, heavy oars.

"You did that. How did you do it?"

"Plastic explosive. I set the charges earlier." He held up his hand so the kid could see Gadgets's device in the light cast by the burning craft. "This triggered the charges."

"I thought you traded my life for yours. In the building. When you got me out of there and didn't tell them I thought you were making a trade." His tone was close to that of one bringing an accusation.

"There was no trade mentioned nor implied. They weren't going to let you go free. I didn't trade for your life. I took it from them."

End of statement. End of philosophy.

Slowly, then with increasing power, the kid again began putting his entire body into the oars. The rhythmic creak of the oars in their locks brought reality back to that portion of the world lighted by the still leaping flames of shattered vessels.

Other than a few initial cries of surprise and pain, those aboard the two doomed boats made no outcry. That part of Bolan's job was done.

The kid hauled at the oars in silence. Sure, Rick had a lot to work out in his mind. It was one thing to read about life and death. The actual reality of the process, in three-dimensional living color, was something else.

And the kid had been wading knee-deep in reality. The shocks to mind and body were enough to knock the pins from under most. Only an inner fiber, tough beyond expectation, could have enabled the kid to hold up thus far.

"What about Becky?"

Before Bolan could frame an answer to this expected question, the night's stillness was shattered by the roar of Big Jim Lane's twin inboards. Bolan's head came up in a listening attitude.

"Twin inboards," Rick hissed.

For the first time the blade of one oar caught the top of a wave. The icy water sprayed the big man.

"Sorry."

Bolan gave no indication he heard the apology or felt the frigid water. His entire attention was centered on the probing finger of light that was preceding the pursuing craft.

Without changing his position on the seat, he turned his head to survey the shore. It was too distant by far. At the rate the needle of electric brilliance was closing in on them it was strictly no contest.

A chatter of .45 Thompson warning filled the air. A shouted command silenced the gunner.

Okay. This might be it. The few seconds that remained offered no hope. If the onrushing craft held even five or six gunners with stutter guns, they were finished. It was that simple.

The kid's breath was coming in sobbing gasps as he put physical reserves on the line.

Careful not to diminish his night vision by looking directly toward the searching spotlight, Bolan readied the big .44 for battle.

Subconsciously he realized the straining diesel to which he had been only half listening was still. Stiles had reached shore. The chances of Bolan and the kid joining him in Kenlandport were so minimal only

Lloyd's would be likely to cover the risk. And they only with great reluctance.

BUD STILES EXPERIENCED A BAD MOMENT when he heard the pair of cabin cruisers break from their shelter. If they were after him he could visualize the outcome of the confrontation.

He gripped the AK-47 and glanced over his shoulder. At that instant the lead cruiser became a flaming marker in the water.

As the tall fisherman tried to understand what had befallen the craft, its mate met a similar fate. The rolling booms of the twin explosions came to Bud across open water.

A broad, unconscious grin came and spread to light his eyes. That big devil! It had to be his doing. Stiles shook his head in a silent gesture of admiration. Who in hell was that guy?

No. Bud did not really want to know who the man was. Some things a man was better off not knowing. All that mattered now was that the unknown warrior was breaking the backs of those who had come to control the lives of most of the residents of tiny Kenlandport.

Aware the wharf was approaching rapidly, Bud throttled back. By the light of the ever brightening moon he caught the silhouette of Tom Devereaux's trawler off to starboard. Tied up for the night at the village's main dock, it lent assurance in a world seemingly gone mad.

But it was over now. The nightmare was at an end.

For the first time in weeks Bud Stiles could suck air into his lungs and again feel like a free man.

As his aging craft eased toward the dock, a figure rose from where it was seated.

"Send me a line, Bud. I'll get you tied up."

Bud cast the line as requested. Hell, how long had it been since someone offered to help him tie up an hour or so before dawn? And especially Wilmer?

Wondering what the wily lobster poacher had in mind, Bud cut the throttle back, reversed, then let the prop pull against the bow line now made fast. It was the easiest docking he had accomplished in a month.

Wilmer cleated the stern line and Bud killed the faithful diesel.

"Thanks." Bud moved toward the rail. "Hold up a second." He turned and took a step toward the under-the-shelf hiding place for the assault rifle he had liberated from the island.

Bud Stiles never saw Wilmer reach for the cutdown twelve. He did hear the twin hammers come back to full cock. For the space of half a heartbeat Stiles struggled mentally to place the metallic sound.

The second half of the beat was lost in the thunderous report as the lead trigger responded to the pressure of Wilmer's thick forefinger.

It was like the time the boom came around on a schooner Bud crewed as a kid. Then, he had feared his back was broken. Now, the same sort of body-wrenching pain took possession of him.

With the AK-47 still in his roughened hand, Bud

swung to face the back-shooter. The assault rifle's muzzle swung toward the man on the dock.

A second time the shortened twelve roared into the night. The load of double-ought ripped and tore their way into the chest of the man aboard the fishing vessel. The force of the pellets straightened Stiles from the crouch he had assumed. Straightened and pressed him back a pace.

The dying man's own finger tightened. The AK-47, on full automatic, chattered its reply to the shotgun's roar. Its 7.62mm missiles ripped and chewed at the sagging dock. A pair of the deadly slugs tore their way into the belly of Wilmer Moore. Clutching himself at the sudden burning agony, the man who would be king of Kenlandport dropped to his knees.

Without ever knowing he had repaid Wilmer, Bud Stiles slumped to the deck of his vessel. There, in silent suffering, his life slowly leaked out on the deck he had walked for so many years.

In the village a dog barked, then was silent. Though residents lay silent and fearful in their beds, not a single fresh light showed. The response to the shooting was silence and an unwillingness to become further entangled in the terror ruling their lives.

Eventually a shadow detached itself from the larger shadow of which it was a part. That shadow became two as the pair of women slowly moved toward the death scene. And, unseen by them, Tom Devereaux moved to better observe what his two women were up to.

The women advanced along the length of the deck. Its uneven surface lent caution to their steps.

The moaning of Wilmer Moore came clearly to them. In the pale light of the fog-free moon, the two saw him curled around his torn belly as he lay hunched on the dock. The injured man rocked from side to side as though by so doing he could quench the fire threatening his very being.

In the light of Wilmer's own flashlight, the two old women studied him.

Wilmer peered into the light with squinting eyes.

"Help me! For the love of God, help me! I'm dying!"

In silence the two studied the nail-furrows that showed like rust streaks on the man's face and through his whiskery stubble.

"Help me! I need help!" he moaned.

"Where's Becky?" Stella's voice was low, scarcely more than a harsh whisper.

For the first time Wilmer was aware of the identity of those who held his flashlight.

"I'm gut shot, Stella. I've got to have help!"

"Where's my granddaughter? Where in thunderation is Becky?"

Despite the pain Wilmer forced his head to move from side to side. "I haven't seen her all day."

Velma's toe found Wilmer's ribs. A gasp of pain slipped from between his lips.

"Oh, God! Don't do that. I hurt something terrible!"

"I'll ask one more time, Wilmer. Where is

Becky?'' The flat finality in Stella's voice decided for him.

"She's out at the farm. Our farm. She's in the barn."

"She'd better be unhurt." Menace so thick it could be cut with a knife filled her voice.

"She's fine. I never intended her harm. Now, help me!"

The two women exchanged a quick glance.

"There's an old wheelbarrow beside that nearest shed. I'll bring it." Velma moved away to bring it without waiting for Stella's response.

A few minutes later the two sisters hoisted and helped the gut-shot man into the barrow. His legs extended to flop on either side of the wheel.

Velma bent and took both handles in her hands. A smile tightened the sagging flesh of her face.

"God bless the two of you."

"Rest yourself, Wilmer. Stella and I will take care of you."

As the procession made its way up the rocky beach, Tom Devereaux considered stopping the slow-moving group. Just as quickly he rejected the thought. It was women's work they were about. Best leave them to it.

Drifting in and out of consciousness, the stricken man lost track of time and direction. When the wheelbarrow came to rest on its rear supports Wilmer forced his eyes open. His nostrils reacted to a familiar smell.

"Just give us a bit of help, Wilmer. We'll get you

onto your feet." Stella's voice was that of an adult soothing a child with a badly skinned knee.

Wilmer willed his legs to cooperate. He shook his head. Something was wrong. Terribly wrong.

"Here we go now. Up you come." Velma's words were indistinct as she strained to aid in moving the man's bulk.

A wooden partition struck his torn belly and brought a grunt of pain. As the two women, working as a team, bent to grasp his feet, realization came to the injured man.

"No!" The protest was torn from his lips as his feet rose. *"No!"*

For a long, terrible second his ripped and savaged belly supported his weight across the top board of the low fence. Eyes open now and seeing, Wilmer was face to face with the reddened eyes of a sow who easily outweighed him by two hundred pounds.

Wilmer's feet described an arc as he plunged head-first into the pen of hungry, angry sows. He forgot the burning pain in his belly as he fought to get his legs under him. The enraged sows gave him all the chance he earlier allowed Bud Stiles.

Drawn by the smell of warm blood, hurt and angered at their recent lack of care, the big-snouted animals were upon him in an instant.

Huge jowls, razorlike teeth, and powerful jaws tore into the living flesh. One sow, the one Wilmer first saw, planted a hoof firmly in his lower ribs and buried her teeth and snout in the bloody warmth of his opened belly.

A second beast nuzzled his upper thighs before ripping into the flesh between them. A howl of animal fear and misery filled the night as his fate struck home.

Desperately, Wilmer tried to beat a third animal away from his face and throat. She grabbed his flailing arm at the wrist. And then Wilmer was trying to beat her away with only a stump from which scarlet spattered and drew the other sows to their feast.

Without looking back, Velma and Stella retraced their steps. Between them they pushed the empty wheelbarrow.

18

Murph O'Reilly held the rocketing craft on course with capable hands. It was not his first time at the helm on a mad dash across the water. Behind the light, Fish braced against the hull chop and quartered the beam across the black water.

"Have you spotted them yet?" Big Jim Lane's voice was such that a listener in Boston could have heard.

"We'll find 'em," Fish assured his boss. "No way they can outrun us."

"When we do I want that big bastard in black. But I want him alive. He's got some questions to answer."

Fish gave no indication he had heard. That sort of thing did not appeal to him. Hell, it didn't set well with any man who was a man. But Big Jim was boss. He called the shots.

On either side of the careening craft armed troops stood ready to do battle. Not counting Big Jim and those at the helm and light, there were eight men aboard. All equipped with automatic weapons. And all ready and eager to draw blood. No man liked having his world kicked to pieces around him. Especially not troops used to doing the kicking.

It was the moon rather than the spotlight that betrayed Bolan and the kid. Both of them heard the excited cry of the hardnose who caught a glimpse of the silver of an oar splash.

Okay, so it came down to this. No need to try for quiet, to hope against desperate hope that shore would arrive in time.

And there was nothing to be gained from retreat. In battle, victory more often than not went to the force that took the conflict to the enemy. Mack Bolan steadied himself as best he could against the motion of the dory and let the .44 thunder a word of warning. At just under a hundred yards the hand-held weapon was as accurate as a rifle. With the frantic dory as a fire base, however, accuracy was something else again.

Even so, the big 240-grain convincer convinced one hardman that the battle was far from won. The bone-crushing mass of metal removed the guy's arm just above the elbow. It was the sort of warning anyone could understand.

Unknowing and uncaring as to who was hit, Big Jim again filled the bay with the sound of his voice.

"Take 'em! Gun 'em down!" All memory that he had just ordered his troops to take at least one of the pair alive vanished. For the moment Big Jim was possessed with a bloodlust.

The sound of automatic weapons filled the night. A hail of lethal slugs peppered the water near and around the dory. A few of the projectiles whined from wave tops and spent themselves in space.

Bolan triggered a trio of booming responses. Of

the three, one spent itself in the boat's hull while a second removed the lower part of an eager hardguy's ear. The third chunk of roaring death found its target. A guy on the port side of the craft lost interest in the quest.

The big slug entered just beneath his lower right rib cage. Due to Bolan's angle at the water level, the slug was traveling upward when it impacted on flesh. Its path took it through the diaphragm and the lower portion of the lung. On exiting, the death-bringer took chunks of five ribs and pieces of spine with it.

When Murph adjusted the helm to bring the craft about slightly, the torn and battered man pitched into the bay. None of his crewmates mourned his passing. It was doubtful any were aware he was no longer with them.

Bolan's next targets centered on the probing light in the bow. Twice he let fly roaring rounds of thunder. And twice his efforts met with success. The first crashed into the light, sending hunks of glass and metal spraying into the night.

The second round was unleashed while the first was still in flight. It took the light's operator squarely beneath the breastbone. The slug's force lifted him back from the light and deposited him at the feet of Big Jim Lane.

In the moon's silvery glow Big Jim gazed down at the dead man who regarded his boss with solemn dead eyes.

Bolan spent the last of the AutoMag's magazine in

an attempt to take out either the helmsman or one of the inboards. His attempt ended in failure.

As the big warrior slapped a fresh clip into the big handgun, the first .45 and 7.62mm seekers found their range. The dory's heavy hull absorbed chunks of punishment, and the oar closest to the onrushing craft lost a portion of its blade in the assault.

Yeah, the numbers were all gone. Totally spent.

"Rick, where's a life jacket?"

"Under that seat you're sitting on," the kid responded.

Bolan located the once-orange jacket by touch and fumbled it free of where it was stuffed for safekeeping.

He knew what needed doing, what had to be done. Whether the vanished numbers would allow it was something else again.

The waxed paper covering of his remaining chunk of plastic explosive was familiar to his touch. The Executioner's powerful thumb and fingers drove the detonator through the paper and deep inside the malleable mass of instant death.

As a cross-sweep of .45-caliber fire filled the water with a line of waterspouts, Bolan extracted his stiletto from a slit pocket and dug the blade's point into the material of the life jacket. The wound in the fabric enlarged as the stiletto's edge parted the material.

Bolan dug a fistful of kapok filling from the life preserver and let it fall to his feet. Into this nest he pressed the chunk of plastic explosive and its inserted detonator. He tossed the jacket and its precious cargo over the dory's stern. A dozen yards astern of their fleeing boat the jacket struck the water.

"Give it all you've got, Rick!"

Something in Bolan's voice urged the youth to maximize his efforts.

Bolan recognized the increase in cadence and appreciated the kid's obedience and stamina. The stained orange life jacket bobbed on the choppy water. The approaching gunnery platform was closing in fast. Now or never time was heartbeats away.

"Hold course, Murph." Big Jim's shouted order carried clearly above the chatter of automatic weaponry. "We'll ram the bastard."

The bellowed command was all Bolan needed. Knowing that the wave-hopping speedster would continue to run dead on, no matter what, he again let the .44 speak for him. Yeah, and for the kid and for Becky wherever she was.

His first pair of heart-stoppers took the fight out of the nearest soldier on the starboard side. While his fellow troops struggled to bring weapons to bear despite the craft's wild bounding from wave crest to wave crest, the latest casualty went overboard.

The combination of bouncing pursuit craft and bobbing dory took the next pair of belly-busters wide of their mark. Beneath him, Bolan felt the dory beginning to yaw. The exhausted kid was fighting the oars in desperation.

The Executioner loosed another one-two pair of 240-grain hell-raisers before giving his total attention to the life jacket. He strained to verify the jacket's position. The pursuing craft relentlessly slammed its way through the choppy water only yards from the life jacket.

The bow waves were just pushing the orange floater to the boat's port side when Bolan thumbed the remote firing indicator. Orange fire erupted from the sea. The racing firing platform came prow up in the water. Moonlight shone through the savaged hull.

Stern-heavy with the two mighty inboards, thrown onto its churning propellers by the blast, the speedster never had a chance. It slipped beneath the water's surface within seconds.

Above the craft's watery grave concussion-shocked troops made confused efforts to remain afloat. Explosion-stunned nonswimmers sank as quickly as did the ravaged boat.

Loyal to the end, Murph O'Reilly struggled through the chill water. Though scarcely conscious himself, Murph managed to get an arm around the neck of his towering boss. The motion briefly pulled Big Jim's mouth and nose underwater.

In blind panic, Big Jim clawed for salvation. For any straw he might clutch in his mindless fear in the icy sea. His right hand found hope. His left joined it. Try as he might Murph was incapable of breaking the stranglehold about his throat. Big Jim Lane pulled his faithful lieutenant down with him without ever knowing that both his massive posts of legs were already at the bottom of the bay.

"Ease off, Rick."

In response the kid shipped the heavy oars. The

solid dory bounced and bobbed in the explosion's wake like a wine cork set adrift. But the staunch dory coped with the rough water.

"Are they all dead?" The words slipped from between the youth's lips as his lungs gulped in the cool air.

"Probably. Those that aren't are keeping a low profile."

Seconds became minutes and still they sat. Bolan might have offered to take the oars but he knew better. The kid brought them out. The kid would take them back. That was the way it should be, had to be.

Eventually, in the pale light of the moon, the kid began to slowly, stoically dip the oars.

19

So the damn fools finally blew themselves to kingdom come. Tom Devereaux emitted a grunt of satisfaction. Only two of them left in the dory. And from the look of it, probably his, Tom's, dory to boot. Now the slightly built guy at the oars was making toward the main dock. Probably thought to liberate Tom's trawler and its hold full of goodies.

He'd blow the larger of the two right out of the dory. Then, by all that was holy, the other could damn well tell him where his grandkid was. And quick, too, unless he wanted to find how it felt to have a foot shot from under him. He cocked the twin hammers of the cut-down twelve that had belonged to Wilmer Moore.

Whoever was at the oars was fixing to run the dory onto the beach. That suited Tom fine. Using an overturned dory for cover he waited patiently. He had all the time in the world. They didn't, but he did.

The big guy must be some sort of diver. He wore the same kind of skintight outfit he'd seen divers wear in the year-round cold waters of coastal Maine. No matter. He reckoned a load of double-ought buck would find its way through the suit.

The big guy hopped into the water and helped the dory onto the stony beach. Then the smaller of the two was on foot and tugging the dory up the shore.

And hell yes, it *was* his dory! Bastards thought they owned Kenlandport. But they did not own Tom Devereaux. He made today's run for Becky. Not out of fear for himself. And now he would help that big so-and-so on his way to hell.

"Stand fast or die!"

Then things happened faster than old Tom intended.

"Tom! It's me, Rick Cartright! Don't shoot!"

And just like that, the guy in black was pointing some sort of hand cannon at Tom's chest. Probably the one he kept blasting out in the bay.

"No!" Rick's voice rose in alarm. "That's Tom Devereaux! Don't kill him!" The youth saw Tom's gun. "Don't shoot, Tom. This man is a friend!"

The group stood unmoving, then Tom realized it really was Rick Cartright. Slowly he eased the pressure on the trigger. When it happened Tom never knew, could not recall later, but when he again glanced at the dark-clad man, the big cannon was riding his hip.

By then Rick was sitting on the edge of the dory with his face buried in his hands.

"I'm John Phoenix," Bolan said as he closed the distance between the two of them, his right arm out.

"Reckon I'm an old fool name of Tom Devereaux."

The strength of Tom's grip belied his years.

WITH THE KID CALLING THE SHOTS, Bolan piloted the car through the lifting dark.

"There it is. The lane entrance is just ahead."

Bolan killed the vehicle's lights and swung into the lane. Scarcely more than two tracks with a weed-grown dividing strip, it led directly toward the darkened house and outbuildings.

"Oh, God, let her be all right." Rick was unaware he spoke aloud.

"Easy," Bolan cautioned as he cut the ignition.

But Rick was free of the car and calling her name as he raced toward the barn.

At a slower pace Mack Bolan followed. Alert, wary, his gaze swept the immediate area missing nothing.

The kid was flinging aside the heavy sliding door as if it were made of cardboard.

"Becky!" He strained to peer into the darkness of the barn.

There was movement just inside the door and to the right. Bolan shot the pencil-thin beam of his pocket flash in that direction.

Her hair was matted with grease and dirt. Wild, dark eyes that could fill with love or hate stared from a grimy face.

Overhead she held a twelve-inch wrench poised to strike in a skull-busting stroke. Slowly, hesitantly, the girl lowered her weapon. It fell beside her bloody foot as she threw herself into the arms of the kid.

Minutes later Becky Devereaux accepted John Phoenix with the same unruffled appraisal as had her grandmother.

She held Rick's hand while Bolan freed the fabric of her jeans from the crusted bruises on her shin. Twice as he cleaned and dressed the gouged shin and foot Becky flinched free of his gentle fingers. And each time she returned her foot to him without having to be told.

Yeah, Rick had guts and to spare. But he was not the only one. Bolan was ready to take any odds offered in favor of their eventual success in life. Any odds at all and cover all bets. And come up a sure winner.

During the return ride to Kenlandport, Becky buried herself in the warmth of the kid's body. Though he was not bound by omens, Mack Bolan was willing to accept the horizon's lightening as a portent of good things to come for these brave kids.

TOM SIPPED AT THE SCALDING, heavily sugared tea and warmed his hands on the cup. Though he pretended disinterest, he cocked his head in a listening attitude each time one of the women went to the living-room window to check on Bolan's still-absent car.

"So who will claim that cargo?" Stella took up the debate.

"Sarah Moore could do with a bit of help. Enough to pay the funeral and maybe sort of get her onto her feet."

"Won't need a funeral. A memorial service will do just fine."

Velma's tone was one of finality. Tom chose not to dispute her words.

"I don't suppose some extra cash would come amiss for Bud's wife and young ones."

Both women indicated their agreement without having to resort to spoken words.

"And I suspect Becky and Rick figure that a table and a couple of chairs and a double bed are all they need to set up housekeeping." Tom's words were dry and crisp.

"And a new kitchen range and a refrigerator for here wouldn't be money wasted."

Tom's suggestion met no opposition.

The sound of a car's motor ended the discussion, and they all hurried outside.

While Becky held her family close, Rick and the man he knew as John Phoenix clasped hands firmly. Finally the girl pulled free.

"The sows. I've got to see to them."

Bolan caught the exchange of glances between the two women.

"I'll be going right past the pen on my way to Portland," he said easily. "Why don't I just give them a couple of buckets of corn. You can check them later."

Two pairs of faded, world-weary eyes caught his and silently thanked him.

"What about water?" Bolan asked through his open window when he got into his car.

"That's all right," Becky told him. "A little spring from up the slope runs through their pen."

The kid seemed to want to say something but did not know how. Bolan gave him an almost grin and a flash of eyes. The kid got the message and returned the grin.

The Executioner set the car to life and eased away from the reunion. He was no longer needed.

Five minutes later he found himself at the pigpen. His first bucket of cracked corn drew most of the sows from where they clustered. His second brought the rest rooting and snorting to the trough. It was only then he got a clear look in the early morning's light.

The Executioner surveyed the scene and wished he had not. Yeah, the sisters would slip away and tidy things up before Becky came out to check on her sows. But he would just as soon they had done the tidying before he arrived.

He returned to the car and eased the emergency brake free.

Every individual had to oppose terror in his or her own way. Or give in to it. The two women in their faded worn dresses used the weapons available to them. And who was he to condemn others for doing what they felt needed doing?

He toed the gas pedal and pointed the vehicle toward the winding dirt road that would eventually join the winding paved road. And eventually the interstate. Along the way he would use a pay phone. Get Jack Grimaldi out of the sack and into the air.

Behind Mack Bolan the coastal village of Kenlandport began life anew. Without giving it further thought, The Executioner toed the pedal a bit more firmly.

MACK BOLAN
THE EXECUTIONER SERIES

I am not their judge, I am their judgment—I am their executioner.
—Mack Bolan,
a.k.a. Col. John Phoenix

Mack Bolan is the free world's leading force in the new Terrorist Wars, defying all terrorists and destroying them piece by piece, using his Vietnam-trained tactics and knowledge of jungle warfare. Bolan's new war is the most exciting series ever to explode into print. You won't want to miss a single word. Start your collection now!

"Today's hottest books for men.... The Executioner series is the grandest of all!"
—*The New York Times*

#39 The New War
#40 Double Crossfire
#41 The Violent Streets
#42 The Iranian Hit
#43 Return to Vietnam
#44 Terrorist Summit
#45 Paramilitary Plot
#46 Bloodsport
#47 Renegade Agent

#48 The Libya Connection
#49 Doomsday Disciples
#50 Brothers in Blood
#51 Vulture's Vengeance
#52 Tuscany Terror
#53 The Invisible Assassins
#54 Mountain Rampage
#55 Paradine's Gauntlet
#56 Island Deathtrap

GOLD
EAGLE

Available wherever paperbacks are sold.

HE'S EXPLOSIVE.
HE'S UNSTOPPABLE.
HE'S MACK BOLAN!

He learned his deadly skills in Vietnam…then put them to use by destroying the Mafia in a blazing one-man war. Now **Mack Bolan** is back to battle new threats to freedom, the enemies of justice and democracy—and he's recruited some high-powered combat teams to help. **Able Team**—Bolan's famous Death Squad, now reborn to tackle urban savagery too vicious for regular law enforcement. And **Phoenix Force**—five extraordinary warriors handpicked by Bolan to fight the dirtiest of anti-terrorist wars around the world.

Fight alongside these three courageous forces for freedom in all-new, pulse-pounding action-adventure novels! Travel to the jungles of South America, the scorching sands of the Sahara and the desolate mountains of Turkey. And feel the pressure and excitement building page after page, with nonstop action that keeps you enthralled until the explosive conclusion! Yes, Mack Bolan and his combat teams are living large…and they'll fight against all odds to protect our way of life!

Now you can have all the new Executioner novels delivered right to your home!

You won't want to miss a single one of these exciting new action-adventures. And you don't have to! Just fill out and mail the coupon following and we'll enter your name in the Executioner home subscription plan. You'll then receive four brand-new action-packed books in the Executioner series every other month, delivered right to your home! You'll get two **Mack Bolan** novels, one **Able Team** and one **Phoenix Force.** No need to worry about sellouts at the bookstore…you'll receive the latest books by mail as soon as they come off the presses. That's four enthralling action novels every other month, featuring all three of the exciting series included in The Executioner library. Mail the card today to start your adventure.

FREE! Mack Bolan bumper sticker.

When we receive your card we'll send your four explosive Executioner novels and, absolutely FREE, a Mack Bolan "Live Large" bumper sticker! This large, colorful bumper sticker will look great on your car, your bulletin board, or anywhere else you want people to know that you like to "Live Large." And you are under no obligation to buy anything—because your first four books come on a 10-day free trial! If you're not thrilled with these four exciting books, just return them to us and you'll owe nothing. The bumper sticker is yours to keep, FREE!

Don't miss a single one of these thrilling novels…mail the card now, while you're thinking about it. And get the Mack Bolan bumper sticker FREE!

BOLAN FIGHTS AGAINST ALL ODDS TO DEFEND FREEDOM!

Mail this coupon today!

Gold Eagle Reader Service, a division of Worldwide Library
In U.S.A.: 2504 W. Southern Avenue, Tempe, Arizona 85282
In Canada: 649 Ontario Street, Stratford, Ontario N5A 6W2

FREE! MACK BOLAN BUMPER STICKER
when you join our home subscription plan.

YES. please send me my first four Executioner novels. and include my FREE
Mack Bolan bumper sticker as a gift. These first four books are mine to examine free for
10 days If I am not entirely satisfied with these books. I will return them within 10 days
and owe nothing If I decide to keep these novels. I will pay just $1.95 per book (total
$7.80) I will then receive the four new Executioner novels every other month as soon
as they come off the presses. and will be billed the same low price of $7.80 per ship-
ment I understand that each shipment will contain two Mack Bolan novels. one Able
Team and one Phoenix Force There are no shipping and handling or any other hidden
charges I may cancel this arrangement at any time. and the bumper sticker is mine to
keep as a FREE gift. even if I do not buy any additional books.

NAME   (PLEASE PRINT)

ADDRESS   APT. NO

CITY   STATE/PROV.   ZIP/POSTAL CODE

Signature   (If under 18. parent or guardian must sign) 166-BPM-PABG

This offer limited to one order per household We reserve the right to exercise discretion in
granting membership If price changes are necessary. you will be notified
Offer expires 29 February 1984.

1. How do you rate _____ ?
   (Please print book TITLE)

   1.6 ☐ excellent   .4 ☐ good   .2 ☐ not so good
   .5 ☐ very good   .3 ☐ fair   .1 ☐ poor

2. How likely are you to purchase another book in this series?

   2.1 ☐ definitely would purchase   .3 ☐ probably would not purchase
   .2 ☐ probably would purchase   .4 ☐ definitely would not purchase

3. How do you compare this book with similar books you usually read?

   3.1 ☐ far better than others   .4 ☐ not as good
   .2 ☐ better than others   .5 ☐ definitely not as good
   .3 ☐ about the same

4. Have you any additional comments about this book?

   _____ (4)
   _____ (6)

5. How did you *first* become aware of this book?

   8. ☐ read other books in series   11. ☐ friend's recommendation
   9. ☐ in-store display   12. ☐ ad inside other books
   10. ☐ TV, radio or magazine ad   13. ☐ other _____
   (please specify)

6. What *most* prompted you to buy this book?

   14. ☐ read other books in series   17. ☐ title   20. ☐ story outline on back
   15. ☐ friend's recommendation   18. ☐ author   21. ☐ read a few pages
   16. ☐ picture on cover   19. ☐ advertising   22. ☐ other _____
   (please specify)

7. What type(s) of paperback fiction have you purchased in the past
   3 months? Approximately how many?

	No. purchased		No. purchased
☐ contemporary romance	(23) ____	☐ espionage	(37) ____
☐ historical romance	(25) ____	☐ western	(39) ____
☐ gothic romance	(27) ____	☐ contemporary novels	(41) ____
☐ romantic suspense	(29) ____	☐ historical novels	(43) ____
☐ mystery	(31) ____	☐ science fiction/fantasy	(45) ____
☐ private eye	(33) ____	☐ occult	(47) ____
☐ action/adventure	(35) ____	☐ other	(49) ____

8. Have you purchased any books from any of these series in the past
   3 months? Approximately how many?

	No. purchased		No. purchased
☐ Mack Bolan (The Executioner)	(51) ____	☐ Phoenix Force	(55) ____
☐ Able Team	(53) ____	☐ Other Adventure series	(57) ____

9. On which date was this book purchased? (59) _____

10. Please indicate your age group and sex.

    61.1 ☐ Male   62.1 ☐ under 15   .3 ☐ 25-34   .5 ☐ 50-64
    .2 ☐ Female   .2 ☐ 15-24   .4 ☐ 35-49   .6 ☐ 65 or older

Thank you for completing and returning this questionnaire.

N1234

PRINTED IN CANADA

NAME _____
(Please Print)

ADDRESS _____

CITY _____

ZIP CODE _____

BUSINESS REPLY MAIL

FIRST CLASS   PERMIT NO. 70   TEMPE, AZ.

POSTAGE WILL BE PAID BY ADDRESSEE

NATIONAL READER SURVEYS

1440 SOUTH PRIEST DRIVE
TEMPE, AZ 85266

NO POSTAGE
STAMP
NECESSARY
IF MAILED
IN THE
UNITED STATES